ALL GIRL 2

LESBIAN EROTICA BUNDLE

VICTORIA RUSH

COPYRIGHT

For the uninhibited...

TURN UP THE HEAT IN YOUR LIFE!

To receive more free books and other steamy stuff, sign up for my newsletter.

Victoria Rush Erotica

VOLUME ONE

WEBCAM CHAT

1

CYBERSURFING

After my playdate with the dominatrix, I felt I needed a breather to regain control over my sex life. My little excursion into the world of BDSM had been fun, but being whipped and hog-tied by a domme had its limits. Now it was *my* turn to set the terms of engagement. I wanted to be back in the driver's seat and branch out beyond one dominant partner.

One lonely night at home, I sat down in front of my computer and began searching for some online fun. I wanted something different from the run-of-the-mill porn—something more engaging. I needed something involving a live, two-way interaction. With a real person, someone with whom I could share a genuine, passionate, if only temporary, relationship. A virtual *fuck buddy*, for want of a better word.

I typed in the search words *webcam sex chat* and a bunch of listings popped up for live online chat. I clicked on one labeled *LiveGirls*, and a gallery of videos showing scantily-clad women touching themselves filled the screen. I tapped one of the thumbnails, where a live stream showed a pretty girl lying facedown on a bed, wearing only a thong. As she swayed her hips from side to side, she looked over her shoulder suggestively toward the camera. Beside the video window, a flurry of comments filled the chat box.

Spread your legs, someone named bigjohn said.

Nice ass, hornyjoe commented.

Can I see your tits? guest34 pleaded.

All the while, the pretty brunette ran her hands across her concealed breasts and rolled her hips in the same robotic manner. For a moment, I was hypnotized like everyone else by her lithe and sexy body. But as attractive as she was, I had no interest in joining what amounted to a public strip show. I was just about to exit the screen when I noticed a button for Private Chat.

Let's see if she's any more engaging one-on-one, I thought.

I clicked the button and a Join Now window covered the stream.

Jeesuz, I cursed. They never make this easy.

I filled in the required fields for Username, Password, and E-mail, then clicked the button. The next screen presented me with a choice between selecting ten free credits or buying a package of credits starting at fifty dollars.

So that's how it works, I thought. *It's not much different from a real strip club. As long as you're stuffing their stockings with cash, the girls are happy to put on a show for you.*

I'd never paid for sex of any kind, and I wasn't about to get started now. I didn't want to chat with someone who was only in it for the money. I backtracked to the main search screen and adjusted my search phrase to *free amateur sex chat* and clicked Enter.

A fresh set of listings popped up, including an intriguing one named *SexRoulette — free webcam live chat*. When I clicked on the link, a window came up with two side-by-side blank video screens. I enabled my laptop cam and mic, then I clicked the Start button. Suddenly, a live feed of me sitting half-naked in my bathrobe appeared in the left window, while some naked guy stroking his dick appeared in the right window.

Horrified to see that my face was showing, I quickly tilted my screen down and cursed out loud.

What's the matter? the naked guy typed in the chat box. *You're very pretty. Can I see your face again?*

I paused for a moment, realizing that he could hear me, then I clicked the microphone button to mute my mic. I wasn't prepared to carry on a live audio conversation with some naked guy. For that matter, I wasn't interested in carrying on a sex chat with *any* man.

I clicked the Next button and a different naked guy appeared with his legs spread wide apart, revealing another erect, throbbing cock. Every time I clicked Next, a different naked man appeared, pulling on his pud. As amusing as I found the experience of scrolling through a bunch of men's penises, the thought of chatting with one of these nameless guys turned my stomach.

Where were all the girls? I thought. *Are only guys interested in naughty online chats?*

I scanned the site and noticed some links across the top for different chat rooms. The default setting was for Mixed, but I could also choose between Guys, Girls, and Couples. Intrigued, I clicked on the Couples link, and a new window popped up showing a woman bobbing her head between a man's knees while his hand typed on a computer keyboard beside him on the bed.

Hi, the man typed in the chat window. *Wanna play?*

I paused for a moment, wondering if it might be fun to watch a hetero couple going at it.

Maybe some other time, I typed, before clicking on the Girls tab.

A new window popped up requiring me to verify that I was over eighteen years of age (*only to view girls??*) then I was redirected to a different website showing the familiar gallery of naked girls from the LiveGirls site. When I clicked on one of the images, a similar video and chat screen appeared. Another pretty young girl perched half-naked on a bed, while a bunch of anonymous viewers made lewd comments, 'tipping' her occasionally with tokens. Whenever anybody tipped her enough tokens, she bent over and waved her ass in front of the camera.

What the fuck? I thought. *Is it only professional girls who want to chat online?*

I clicked out of the website and was about to pull my vibrator out of my nightstand for some quiet alone time, when I decided to give it one last try.

There's got to be other lonely girls who are looking for a quick hookup with like-minded women.

I went back to the main search page and typed in *lesbian online chat*. Near the top of the listings, I noticed a site titled *SapphicChat — girls only free online chat.*

That's what I'm talking about, I said out loud, clicking the link.

Another side-by-side video setup appeared on the screen with a chat box underneath. I enabled my cam and carefully positioned my laptop lid so that only my torso was visible, then I pulled my robe tightly around my neck to cover myself up. There'd be no more skin showing until I was able to qualify a suitable candidate.

I clicked the Start button, and within a few seconds the adjacent window flickered with a live stream showing a fat woman lying on her bed with her droopy boobs hanging down by her waist.

Yikes, I said, quickly clicking the Next button. I felt bad judging the visitors so harshly, but it wasn't much different from other dating apps. If you didn't feel the chemistry right away, everybody just moved on.

After a few seconds, a new image filled the sender window. This time an older woman sat in front of her computer with her elbows propped up on her desk. Deep folds of flesh hung from her neck and upper chest as she peered sadly into the screen.

Wow, I thought. *These online forums really bring out the lonely girls.*

I toggled through the list of online visitors until an image appeared showing a younger girl sitting cross-legged on her bed, wearing a tight V-neck sweater. Her breasts were full and plump, and although her face was partially hidden off-screen, I could tell from the downiness of her bare legs in a mid-thigh skirt that she was considerably younger than me. I parted my legs unconsciously as my pussy throbbed in excitement.

Finally. A sexy girl who wants an authentic online chat.

ASL? I typed, wanting to be sure she was of legal age. The last thing I needed was to have the police breaking down my door for engaging a minor in online sex.

19, curious, Houston, she typed. *You?*

Nineteen? She barely looked of age. I'd have to vet her more carefully if things went much further.

I paused for a moment, wondering how I wanted to present myself. I didn't want to scare her away by revealing my true age if she was looking to hook up with someone younger. But she had to lean at least a little bit toward girls if she'd engaged me this far.

28, bi, Milwaukee, I stretched the facts on all three aspects.

She paused for a moment holding her hand over her computer keyboard, then the video screen suddenly went blank and a new visitor came online.

Touché, I thought. *I guess this works both ways. My fellow online surfers can be just as rash and judgmental as me when it comes to who they find attractive.*

Obviously. I hadn't measured up in her eyes. But had I been too old, not the right sexual orientation, or was it my *body* she didn't like?

I peered at my image in my webcam feed and looked at my tightly-bound boobs wrapped up in my bathrobe. I'd been slouching a bit, and the heavy terrycloth robe wasn't doing much justice to the shape of my bosom. I spread the lapels of my robe a few inches apart and lifted my chest. My ample cleavage shone through the opening, revealing the roundness of my breasts.

That looks better, I smiled, nodding at the sexy reflection. *If this doesn't hook them, I'm really losing my mojo.*

The next visitor appeared to be another young girl seated on a chair in front of her computer. She only showed the lower half of her face, but from her tight skin and smooth neck muscles, she looked to be in her late teens or early twenties. Her tight T-shirt had a wish-bone-shaped "C" emblem on the front. In the background, two small double beds sat on either side of her small room.

Hi, I typed, deciding to take a more measured approach with this new visitor. *What brings you to this crazy place so late at night?*

Just bored I guess, she responded.

Me too, I said. *This is my first time doing something like this. I'm used to meeting people the old-fashioned way.*

Boys or girls? she typed.

It was obvious that she was fishing. I had no idea what the right answer was, so I decided to play it safe.

Both, I guess. *But I prefer girls. How about you?*

I like boys... she typed. *But lately I've been finding myself unusually attracted to my dorm mate.*

Oh, I said, happy to hear she tilted both ways. *Where do you go to school?*

University of Chicago.

My heart skipped a beat when I realized how close she was to me in the real world.

What are you studying? I said, trying to steady my nervous hand as I typed.

I'm enrolled in the BA program, so right now it's mostly liberal arts. I'm just in my first year, so I haven't really decided on my major yet. I'm thinking maybe Communications...

She's barely eighteen! I thought. *My pussy throbbed at the thought of uncovering more of this pretty co-ed.*

What kind of career were you thinking of?

I dunno. Public relations, marketing, maybe television.

On the production side?

I suppose so. Somewhere behind the camera. I don't think I have prime time face.

You should let other people be the judge of that. From what I can see so far, I think you're very pretty. The combination of good looks and good communication skills will give you quite a leg up in that field.

Thanks, she said, tilting the camera up a little higher on her face. She smiled a broad smile, revealing perfectly-straight, pearly-white teeth. *What about you, what do you do?*

I'm a freelance graphic designer.

So you design websites and stuff like that?

A little bit of that. But I do more corporate work like logos, editorial layouts, that sort of thing.

That sounds interesting, the girl said. *I guess we both have an interest in communications of sorts...*

I paused for a moment, wondering how much longer I wanted to focus on the professional sides of our lives.

It looks like we share an interest in another form of communicating too. ;-)

LOL. This isn't the kind of communications my profs talk about.

I'm a little surprised to hear that, I said. *The world is rapidly adopting new forms of social media every day. Perhaps you can consider this as a type of vocational training.*

Except most people who come to this website are interested in only one thing.

You mean meeting people? I teased.

In a manner of speaking...

Are you testing the waters here because of your roommate?

Maybe. I didn't realize I had such a strong attraction to girls until I met her.

Have you shared your feelings with her?

Gawd no. She has a boyfriend. It could get very uncomfortable around here if I came on to her too strongly. We have to share this small room for the rest of the year and perhaps for the rest of our college residency.

Two charged up bodies in a small space can make for a combustible mixture. Do you think she's attracted to you also?

Not by the way I've seen her and her boyfriend go at it. I can't tell you how many times I've come back to my room to find a sock on the door.

Poor thing, I thought. *It doesn't sound like she's got much of an outlet to express her real feelings. I better tread lightly.*

Maybe you just need to be a little more suggestive when you have some alone time with her. You know, wear skimpier clothes to bed, come back from the shower naked. That sort of thing. If she's interested, she'll soon let you know.

It sounds like you have a little more experience with girls, she said. *Are you lesbian?*

Now we're getting to the crux of it, I thought. It was kind of fun playing the role of the girl's online mentor.

They say everyone's somewhere on the continuum, I said. *I'd say I'm about a nine, but I seem to be moving more to the right with each passing year. Men don't really do it for me any longer.*

The chat window paused for a moment as the girl seemed to process what I said.

What's it like? she said. *You know, being with a woman?*

Crikey, I thought. *How do I answer that without sounding like some kind of stalker?*

That's an interesting question. It's different in so many ways. Woman like different things than men. We're more focused on building the relation- ship. Men are mostly just interested in sex.

Aren't women interested in that too?

Yes, of course, I laughed. *We just let it happen more—organically.*

Organically?

We let it happen naturally, as our feelings for one another grow stronger. Instead of just jumping on the biscuit, in a manner of speaking.

You mean kind of like what we're doing right now?

I was beginning to feel a strange attraction to this girl. Beyond the pretty outside package, she had a sweet innocence to her.

I suppose, I said. *We lesbians generally like to get to know our partner a little better before jumping into bed with them.*

Do you mind my asking how that works when you do get together? I mean, it's not like regular boy-girl coupling...

All this tip-toeing around the edges of sexy talk was beginning to stir some new feelings inside me. I was enjoying the process of educating this young girl on the nuances of lesbian relationships.

It's not so different, when it comes right down to it. We have the same sensitive parts. We just use them a little differently.

Do you miss the penetration aspect of the relationship?

Maybe it's time to stop being so nuanced, I thought.

Who says we have to forego the penetration aspect?

Oh, sorry—the girl said, as I saw a flush roll over her face. *It's just that without a penis involved in the equation...*

There are lots of ways us girls can enjoy penetration without a man.

Strap-on dildos, two-sided phalluses, using sex toys. I'm guessing you've tried one or two of these before?

Well, yes. I have a vibrator I play with when my roommate is away. But I had no idea women used them together like you said.

Oh, yes. There are lots of interesting ways we make our own fun.

You're getting me pretty worked up talking about it. Can you tell me how you use a two-sided phallus?

Suddenly I became acutely aware of the wetness that had been accumulating between my legs. This innocent but sexy banter had been getting *both* of us worked up.

Well, usually it starts with us lying on our backs with our butts facing one another...

Mmm, the girl typed.

Fuck! I thought. *It's happening. I'm actually seducing a young college girl online!*

Then we insert the two ends in each of our pussies and push our bodies together...

The girl's left hand wandered below my line of vision as she began to squirm in her seat while pecking her keyboard with her other hand.

All the way? she asked. *Do you touch your bodies together?*

Usually, if the dildo isn't too long. That's where it really gets fun. There's nothing so electrifying as feeling your lover's peachka pressed up against your own.

God, that's so hot!

And wet. ;-)

You're making me very wet right now.

I spread my legs and began strumming my clit with my fingers at the thought of the pretty co-ed getting turned on by my explanation.

Are you touching yourself? I said.

Yes. Are you?

I am now.

I wish I could touch you the way you're describing right now.

If I could reach out through my screen, believe me, I would. I'd love to show you what it feels like to make love to a woman.

Can I see your breasts? They look very full and sexy.

I thought you'd never ask.

I pulled my robe apart and let the shawl fall around my shoulders.

OMG! the girl typed. *They're gorgeous. Do you mind if I ask how old you are? Because those are the most beautiful tits I think I've ever seen.*

I paused for a moment trying to decide how young I wanted to pretend to be. The last thing I wanted to do in the heat of the action was scare away another online partner because she thought I was too old.

Everybody tells me I look ten years younger than my real age, I thought. *She'll never know.*

That's very kind of you, I said. *I'm twenty-five. But before we go any further, I should probably ask you the same. If you're in your first year of college, you must be barely legal.*

I turned eighteen two months ago.

Like I said. Barely legal.

We're two consenting adults.

Since we're getting to know each other so intimately, can I ask your name? I don't want to have sex with a faceless, nameless person.

I'm Holly.

Pleased to meet you Holly. My name's Jade.

That's a lovely name.

Yours too, I said. *Holly and Jade. I like the way they go together.*

I'm imagining us going together in more ways than one.

Damn, girl, you're making me soaking wet. Can I see a bit more of you too? I want to let my mind run all over your sweet body.

The girl reached up over her shoulders and pulled her T-shirt over her head. Then she reached behind her back and unclasped her bra. When she pulled it off her shoulders and threw it on the floor, I gasped. Her breasts were smaller than mine, but stood firm and erect on her chest. But far more fascinating, was their *shape*. They were far pointier than most, pressing straight out toward me like two fleshy obelisks.

Mmm, I typed. *Those are mighty succulent boobies you have, Holly.*

Not as full and appetizing as yours! she returned.

I love their shape. I could suck on your pointy nipples all day!

I'd like that, Holly said. *You're going to make me cum pretty soon if you keep talking to me like that.*

That's not the only part of you that I want to suck, I said, starting to rub my clit more quickly. *I want to take your sweet nub into my mouth and watch your twist all over my face.*

Yes, Jade. I want you to suck my clit. Make me cum all over your face.

Oh Baby, I said. *Let me see and feel you cum. I'm pressing my fingers inside you now...*

Fuck, Jade. I can feel you inside me. I'm going to cum...

As I watched Holly writhing in her chair, my mouth opened unconsciously, imagining her riding my face.

Yes, baby, I said. *Cum in my mouth. Let it go.*

Suddenly, a deep flush spread over Holly's chest and she began jerking wildly in her chair.

Ohhhhhhh, she typed. *I'm cumming Jade!*

I hadn't been concentrating very much on my own feelings up to this point, but when I saw Holly coming, I thrust my fingers deep into my pussy and gushed all over my hand. While I watched her jerking in her chair, my tits jiggled spastically on my chest as the tremors spread throughout my body.

After a long pause, Holly began to type again.

That was incredible! she said. *I haven't had an orgasm that powerful in a long time.*

You should try this girl thing more often, I typed. *It's even better in real life. Maybe you and your roommate can find a way—*

Suddenly, Holly's face turned to the side and a panicked expression fell over her face.

I think she's here! she typed. *Someone's at the door!*

Oh no—not now, I thought. *Just when we were establishing such a strong connection.* I banged away at my keyboard, fearful of losing her forever.

Can we do this again some—

Holly's video stream suddenly went dark as she signed out of the program. I was sad to see her go, but at the same time I was thrilled to have made such an exhilarating connection my first time online.

I'm going to have to try this again very soon, I thought, closing my laptop with sticky fingers.

2

———————

FULL DISCLOSURE

After my chat with Holly ended so abruptly, I stayed online for more than an hour hoping she'd reconnect and continue our conversation. But I knew that if her roommate had returned to their dorm, she'd be hard-pressed to find any privacy for the rest of the night. Their single room was so tiny that it would be impossible to find any place for a private conversation, let alone an online sex chat.

For the rest of the night, I fantasized about her roommate barging in to find her masturbating in front of her computer, then tearing off her clothes to join the innocent college girl in her lesbian discovery. If anything could persuade a straight girl to stray to the other side, surely it would be the sight of the winsome co-ed getting off watching other naked women. I came many times that night imagining all the fun the two of them might have discovering the joys of lesbian love-making for the first time.

The following night, I was eager to get back online to see if I could reconnect with Holly. Even though I knew my chances were slim, if she found herself alone again and was in a similar frame of mind, I hoped she might have the same idea. Around the same time that evening, I logged back into the SapphicChat site and began toggling through the gallery of online visitors.

I found a few interesting candidates, and for a short time I engaged in some playful banter with a closeted housewife from Texas, then a curious divorcée from California, then a sexy dyke from Delaware. On any other day, I might have been enticed to remove my clothing and begin another erotic online encounter, but after a few minutes of superficial conversation, I found myself clicking the Next button in search of my innocent college girl.

I was just about to reengage with the Texas housewife when a familiar silhouette filled the visitor chat window. She was sitting cross-legged in the middle of her bed wearing a tight T-shirt and shorts with her face out of the frame, but I recognized the contour of her breasts instantly. Her pointy tits pressed against the soft fabric of her shirt, barely concealing the two tubers of mouthwatering flesh. My pussy throbbed at the sight of the familiar swellings.

Holly? I typed on my keyboard.

Who's this? she responded in the chat box. I was wearing a different outfit this evening, and with my face off-camera, it was obvious she didn't recognize me.

It's Jade. I've been thinking about you so much since our chat last night.

She stretched her legs out on opposite sides of her laptop and leaned her body forward to type on her keyboard. This only accentuated the elongated shape of her breasts, highlighting the meaty areolas at their tips.

Me too. I wasn't sure if I'd find you again. Sorry for cutting you off so suddenly last night.

I completely understand. Did your roommate catch you in the act?

I was able to get myself pulled together pretty quickly. But she must have sensed something was up from the look on my face. Plus, I'm sure the room was saturated with the scent of my sex by the time we finished.

The thought of Holly's scent filling the room made my pussy weep, and I spread my legs unconsciously, feeling the moisture between my legs.

Did you tell her what you'd been doing?

No, I made up some lame-ass excuse about researching a term paper.

Too bad. If anything might swing her the other way, it would be the sight of her pretty roommate getting off watching other girls.

I dunno. I'm still afraid what she might think. I could smell her boyfriend's cologne all over her when she came back. I don't think she's interested in me that way.

Give it time. It's still early in the semester. She probably just needs to get a bit more comfortable around you. Your irresistible personality will eventually win her over.

So you're saying my body's not enough? ;-)

Don't be silly. Your figure is exquisite. I paused for a moment, contemplating whether to take our online conversation to the next level. *Though I still haven't seen your entire face. Don't you think we've come far enough to show the rest of our bodies to one another?*

Holly hesitated with her hands over her keyboard. For a moment, I thought she might hit the Exit button in fear of revealing her real identity.

I guess so, she said. *But I'm kind of wary about my showing my face in a public forum like this. You never know who might be recording us. I'd be horrified if somebody posted this online and my parents saw a clip of me masturbating online one day.*

I know how you feel, I typed. *I've been having the same concerns. Why don't we open a separate private chat. Do you have Skype?*

Yes, Holly said. *I use it to chat with my folks every couple of weeks.*

What's your username? Mine's gigi84.

Is that the year you were born? I thought you said you were twenty-five!

Ok, full disclosure, I sheepishly typed. *I might have stretched my age a little bit. But everyone tells me I look much younger than I really am.*

It's cool, Holly said. *Everybody has a secret identity online. I never would have guessed your age. You certainly have the body of a 25 yr old!*

Sexy enough to entice a college girl into an online affair with a middle-aged woman?

That's not middle-aged! You're barely through the first trimester. But to answer your question, yes. My Skype ID is ucgrad22.

LOL. I'm trying to slow down the clock and you're already looking ahead. Shall we log out of here and start a new Skype chat?

C u in a few minutes, sexy momma! Holly said, signing off with a playful kissing emoji.

As her image disappeared from the video window, my pussy pitter-pattered at her playful description of me. I couldn't wait to have her all to myself on a private webcam link, and I quickly exited the webpage and signed into Skype. I searched for *ucgrad22* and a profile pulled up with a thumbnail image of a pretty teenager wearing sunglasses against a seaside background. I clicked on the image and a new chat window opened, giving me three options. I could leave a text message in the chat box at the bottom of the screen, or I could send her an audio or video call request.

What the hell, I thought. *I think we're well past the preliminaries.*

I tapped on the video button and as my video stream went live, the sound of an electronic call warbled through my speakers. While I waited for Holly to pick up on the other end, I adjusted the angle of my camera so that it focused with a close-up of my face. I'd chosen to wear some skimpy lingerie this evening, and I didn't want to be too presumptuous right out of the gate. Besides, I was eager to see Holly's full face, and I figured if I set the tone, that she might follow.

After a few seconds, the bottom half of the screen filled with the familiar image of Holly's chest in her tight T-shirt. I smiled when I saw her, and she quickly tilted her screen up so that I could see her face also. My heart immediately began accelerating, not only because she appeared so close, but also because she was absolutely stunning. She had large doe-eyes, a cute upturned nose, and long auburn hair falling over her shoulders. With her bright green eyes and sprinkling of little freckles, she looked like a dead-ringer for the actress Emma Stone.

"Can you hear me?" I spoke toward my laptop's onboard microphone.

"Yes," Holly replied. "Oh my God, Jade—you're gorgeous!"

"Not bad for a thirty-five-year-old?" I smiled.

"Not bad for a twenty-five-year-old!" Holly beamed back at me.

"You're not too shabby yourself, young lady," I said. "Those eyes are to die for. Has anyone ever told you that you look a bit like—"

"Yes, I know. Emma Stone. I get it all the time. I think it's just the red hair and freckles. We gingers are always getting compared to one another. Amy Adams, Bryce Howard, Lindsay Lohan—I've heard them all."

"Sorry," I said. "I didn't mean to compare you to anybody. You're gorgeous and unique in your own right."

"No worries. It's just that I used to get teased quite a lot when I was younger."

"Not so much anymore, I bet."

"Thankfully, I seem to be outgrowing it."

"I bet you turn a lot of heads from both boys and girls on campus."

"I haven't been paying much attention. I've been focusing primarily on my studies. I don't get out much..."

"Oh my God, girl. You don't know what you're missing. With a face and body like that, you could have your pick of the litter. You could make your roommate super-jealous by bringing home a hot new boyfriend every night of the week."

"Except I'm not really into guys right now. Though I will confess, I *was* fantasizing about phalluses most of the night."

"Oh? Do tell. Real or pretend ones?"

"All your talk about strap-on dildos and double-sided cocks got me worked up all night. As soon as Jen left in the morning, I took out my vibrator and have been playing with it most of the day."

My pussy throbbed at the thought of Holly jilling herself with a dildo, as I felt a dribble of lubrication run down the crack of my ass.

"Same here. Do you have a favorite?"

Holly leaned over her bed and reached into the night table beside her bed. She pulled out a plain flesh-colored plastic dildo and held it in front of the screen for me to see.

"I just have this one. I actually pulled it out of the trash can at my house a few years ago. I think it belonged to my mother. I've been too nervous to go to an adult store to look for one of my own."

"Jeesuz, girl," I said, staring at the prehistoric sex toy. "That looks like something straight out of the eighties. Vibrators have become a lot more sophisticated over the last few years."

I reached into my side table and pulled out my favorite rabbit vibrator and held it up for Holly to see.

"This is one of my favorites. It's called The Rabbit. It twists and rolls on the end to provide an exquisite form of internal stimulation. But best of all are these little rabbit ears."

I tweaked the two silicone flaps with my fingers.

"When you turn it on, they vibrate and flap directly against your clitoris, providing the most intense type of stimulation you can imagine. The whole thing is made of super-soft silicone, so it almost feels like the real thing when it's inside you."

Holly stared at the multi-colored vibrator with wide eyes, then glanced back at her plain plastic dildo.

"I'm feeling pretty inadequate right now. Can you show me how it works? I mean—just turn it on so I can see how it moves?"

"Of course," I said, happy to indulge Holly's curiosity.

I held the vibrator vertical and turned it sideways so she could see the rabbit ears in profile view, then turned the device on. As it began making a low humming sound, a circle of beads swirled just under the transparent surface.

"See these circulating beads? They provide a sensation unlike any man can deliver."

Emma stared at the strange contraption and nodded.

"I can imagine. How else does it move?"

I pressed another button, and the tip of the dildo started rolling in small circles.

"Holy shit!" Holly exclaimed, with wide eyes. "That thing really is unlike any other cock, isn't it?"

"So you *have* experienced a real penis, then?" I said, probing for more details about her sex life.

"Well yes, just a few times in high school with a boyfriend in my senior year. But he wasn't endowed nearly as well as that thing!"

"It's a little bigger than most men's cocks, I suppose. But here's the best part." I tapped another button on the base of the vibrator and the rabbit ears started fluttering against the side of the shaft. "Can you see that," I said, pointing toward the flickering ears. "That's something else no man's cock can hope to emulate. The combined effect of these three actions will send you over the moon."

"Oh my God," Holly said. "I'm already soaking wet at the thought of having that thing inside me. I don't suppose you'd be willing to demonstrate it working for real? I mean—*inside* you?"

By this time, the insides of my thighs were coated with slippery lubrication emanating from my pussy and my clit was burning in need of some direct stimulation.

"It would be my pleasure—literally."

I unplugged my laptop and carried it with my vibrator to my bed. Then I sat up with my back resting against the headboard and placed the laptop between my legs about two feet away so Holly could see my entire body from my hips to my head.

"Mmm, I like what you're wearing tonight," Holly said, admiring my lacy camisole and matching boy-shorts panties.

"I wore it just for you," I purred, cupping my breasts and pinching my nipples through the thin fabric.

"I wish I were there to touch you like that. I want to caress every square inch of your body."

"Likewise," I said, spreading my legs further apart. "Can you take your T-shirt off so I can see your beautiful breasts while I play with myself? I've been fantasizing about seeing you naked again for the last twenty-four hours."

"Absolutely," Holly said. "In fact, let me get completely naked so I can enjoy myself properly while I'm watching you."

Holly pulled her shirt over her head as her pointy tits jiggled on her chest. Then she raised her ass and pulled her shorts over her ankles, revealing a completely bare pussy.

"Oh my God, Holly," I gasped, staring at her sexy slit and puffy labia. "Just when I thought you couldn't get any more perfect. That might be the prettiest pussy I've ever seen."

"I bet you say that to all the girls," she teased.

"I have to admit that I love every woman's vulva. But yours looks unusually—*pristine*. Almost like it's never been touched. Are you sure you've been with boys before?"

"Only a few times," Holly laughed. "Not as many times as I've used my vibrator."

"Well that skinny little thing isn't much thicker than a toothbrush. No wonder you look like you've barely been touched down there."

"My boyfriend in high school was pretty small too. I didn't know they came any bigger. Show me how that big dildo fills you up, Jade."

I had planned on giving Holly a slow striptease to get her in the mood, but when started talking dirty, I practically tore my panties and camisole off.

Holly paused for a moment as her eyes darted over her screen, appraising my body.

"Holy fuck, Jade! *You're* the one with the perfect body. I'd die to have your curves. You look like something straight out of some men's magazine centerfold."

"Or *women's*," I chuckled. "Hopefully this body works for both sides of the aisle."

Holly traced her right hand down the front of her stomach and began circling her fingers over her clit.

"It's definitely working *this* side of the aisle, I can assure you."

"Mmm, Holly, you're making me very wet."

"Wet enough for that big dildo to slide up inside you?"

"Let's see," I said, placing the end of the vibrator against my opening. I tapped the oscillating function button and the tip of the dildo began rolling over my slippery labia. As I began to insert the dildo inside my hole, Holly leaned in closer to the screen.

"Damn," she panted. "My boyfriend's cock never did anything like that. It was mostly straight in-and-out action. Usually pretty fast."

"You have no idea how good real lovemaking can be," I purred. "The trick is to take your time and let the passion slowly build. Only after you've been properly teased and stimulated, is it time for a pounding. The pleasure is so much more intense when you let it build to a boil."

"You're sure bringing me to a boil right now," Holly said, rolling her fingers over her slit. "Show me how you enjoy the rest of that special dildo. I want to watch you squirm and moan."

I raised my knees higher off the bed and tapped the second button on the vibrator. As the rotating silver beads glistened in the nightlight from my side table, the shaft slowly disappeared inside my cavern as I pushed it further inside me.

"Fuck that's hot!" Holly panted, her big doe eyes widening even further. "What does that feel like inside you?"

"It's like nothing else," I moaned. "The feeling of the beads caressing the inside of my walls while the rotating tip presses against my G-spot is simply indescribable. You've got to get one of these for yourself to truly appreciate it."

"I'll be going to my corner sex shop as soon as it opens tomorrow," Holly grunted, slipping her fingers inside her pussy. "You've certainly sold me."

"Just don't get too attached to it," I said. "It's still doesn't compare to the delicate touch of a real live, sensuous woman."

"But you said I can *combine* both sensations, with the right kind of vibrator. I might buy me one of those two-sided dildos while I'm at the store, just in case the opportunity ever arises with my roommate..."

With that image dancing around my head, I shoved the vibrator deep inside me and tapped on the rabbit ears button. As the ears began flapping against my burning clit, I humped my hips forward and back, pressing the dildo in and out of me.

"That's a sight I'd love to see," I panted, feeling the vibrations emanating throughout my body.

"I'll see if it can be arranged," Holly said, suddenly picking up her plastic vibrator and thrusting it inside her. "That is, if I can ever get past first base with her. I bet she'd enjoy watching you as much as I do. Maybe we can arrange our own little ménage à trois."

"Without her boyfriend, you mean?"

"*Definitely* without him," Holly moaned. "No boys allowed."

Holly and I watched each other holding our dildos with two hands as we fucked ourselves with increasing urgency.

"I'd like that," I panted. "But not nearly as much as being there for real. I want to feel your body pressed up against mine and make you scream in pleasure."

"You're getting pretty close to making me do that right now," Holly moaned, rolling her hips while she stared at her screen. "I'm getting close. Do you think you can cum with me?"

"Fuck yes," I grunted. "Any time. Just tell me when."

"First tell me what you want to do with me. When we get together."

"Oh Holly," I moaned, daring myself to think the unthinkable. "Everything. I want to kiss you and suck you and fuck you with every ounce of my being. We'll take our time and make it last. I'd make love to you all day long if I could."

"How do you want to fuck me, Jade?" Holly panted as her body began tensing up. The pupils in her eyes had become large and dark, signaling that she was nearing her peak. "Will you fuck me with your strap-on dildo or two-headed prick?"

"Yes," I moaned, getting even more turned on by her dirty talk. "I'll fuck you until you come all over my big dildo. I'll make you gush all over my cock while I fuck you in every imaginable way—"

"Yes, Jade," Holly groaned. "I want to feel you inside me. Make me cum all over your big dildo."

Holly was humping her hips wildly now against her plastic dildo, pumping it in and out of her pussy as her breathing became more jagged. I pressed the vibrating rabbit ears hard up against my clit and thrust my vibrator as deep inside me as I could. Within seconds, I could feel the insides of my pussy beginning to expand in preparation for a hard orgasm.

"Cum for me, baby," I groaned, feeling the first waves of passion roll over me. "Press your pussy against me and cum with me. I feel you Holly—"

"Jade!" Holly suddenly screamed, as her hips started shaking in spastic spasms. "I'm cumming!"

Her whole body began convulsing as her pointy breasts shook in tiny tremors.

"Oh baby," I growled, extending my tongue trying to reach her jiggling tits. "Mummy's coming with you. Feel me filling you up. Cum all over my big cock. Let me feel your tight pussy clamping down on me."

"Fuck yes," Holly hissed, holding her spear tightly inside her while her hips convulsed on the bed in front of her computer screen. "I'm still cumming. Oh Jade—"

Suddenly I heard the sound of a door swinging open and another girl's voice.

"What the fuck?" the girl's voice said. "I'm so sorry, Holly. I'll come back later—"

"No," Holly pleaded, peering up from the screen. "Don't leave, Jen. I've been thinking of you..."

Holly glanced down at her screen and gave me a sweet smile, then her video suddenly went blank.

Maybe she'll be getting her wish sooner than she hoped, I thought, pulling the still-throbbing vibrator out of my pussy.

3

THREE'S A CROWD

For the longest time, I stared at the empty screen, imagining what was happening in Holly's dorm room. Her roommate had surprised her in the throes of orgasm, with her naked body splayed in front of her computer and a vibrator deeply embedded in her pussy. How could anyone respond to such a sight?

There were only three possible scenarios. Either her roommate had turned tail and quickly exited the room, closing the door behind her. Or she'd continued into the dorm and gone about her usual business, pretending nothing unusual had happened. Or she'd engaged Holly directly in some way, acknowledging what she'd witnessed. It couldn't be that unusual to discover your roommate masturbating privately in the small confines of the same room. These were young women in the sexual prime of their lives. Where else could they act on their private passions but in the relative seclusion of their own room?

Holly had reached out to her friend in a vulnerable moment. Had her roommate simply brushed it off as a common practice among people their age and told Holly not to worry about it? Or had they begun a meaningful dialogue about Holly's attraction to Jen and discussed whether the feeling was mutual? Or had Jen torn off her *own* clothes and jumped into bed with Holly to begin a torrid affair?

Either way, I couldn't stop thinking about it all night. I came over and over again imagining Jen sucking on Holly's pointy nipples and probing every recess of her with her body. I wondered if Holly had been serious about running out to her local sex shop and stocking up on the latest generation of toys. The thought of she and Jen twisting their bodies together while connected by a two-sided dildo was too much. I plunged my rabbit vibrator back inside my pussy and held it tightly against my mound as I gushed all over the animated phallus.

The following night, I didn't know what to expect. If Jen had responded positively to her outreach, Holly could quickly lose interest in further contact with me. And if her roommate had shunned her advances, she might be reluctant to go back online for fear of being caught in the act again. She might even have trouble finding alone time this late at night. Her roommate couldn't be spending *all* of her free time with her boyfriend. She'd still need time to study and get caught up on her private affairs.

But there was one thing Holly said that kept me coming back. She'd alluded to the possibility of including her roommate in our online games if she got that far. *I'll see if that can be arranged,* she said. I wondered if she meant to go so far as to arrange an in-the-flesh get-together. *Maybe we can arrange our own little ménage à trois.* I'd never been with two girls at the same time, and the possibilities with three women made my head spin.

Around the same time the following evening, I logged back onto SapphicChat to see if she was still available. For over an hour, I toggled through the gallery of online visitors, but there was no sign of Holly. As sexy as some of the other candidates seemed, I had no interest in engaging with anyone else right now. There was only one person I was interested in, and my pretty college girl from UC was nowhere to be found.

I was just about to close my laptop for the night when it suddenly struck me. Maybe Holly had the same idea as me. Maybe she had no interest in wading through another collection of online strangers until she found me again. There was a good chance she was waiting for me to reconnect on our private line, via Skype. I quickly logged out of the public chatroom and launched the private app. When I logged back in, I filtered my list of contacts to display only those who were *Active Now.* Holly's familiar thumbnail appeared with a green dot beside it to indicate that she was online.

Oh my God! I thought. *She's been waiting for me!*

As my pussy fluttered in excitement, I hesitated before sending her a note.

What should I wear for this chat? What if she was with her roommate this time?

I didn't want to be too presumptuous by wearing something too skimpy and come off as some kind of floozy. What if she just wanted to chat to tell me she'd found a new outlet for her lesbian affections?

I went into my wardrobe and wrapped a silk robe over my camisole, then carried my laptop to my bed and made myself comfortable against the headboard. I paused with my hands over my keyboard, wondering how I should proceed after our last embarrassing incident. I decided to send her a text message this time, just to make sure she was free to talk.

Hi Holly, I typed. It's Jade. *Are you alone?*

Within seconds, a video call request came warbling over the line, indicating that she wanted to chat live.

Maybe I didn't scare her off so badly last time after all, I thought, clicking the Accept button.

When the call connected and our video windows went live, this time I saw Holly sitting on the bed next to another young girl wearing a UC T-shirt and skimpy panties.

My heart skipped a beat when I realized what was happening.

Could it really be? I thought. *Had she connected that quickly with her roomie and persuaded her to pull me into their affair?*

"I see you've made a new friend," I spoke into the mic, trying to conceal the excitement in my voice.

"Hi Jade," the other girl said. She appeared to be about Holly's age, and almost as pretty. With long blond hair, penetrating blue eyes, and plump rosebud lips, the pair of them looked like models straight out of an Abercrombie & Fitch commercial. "Holly's told me so much about you."

"Oh?" I said, still dumbfounded at the situation I found myself in.

"This is my roommate Jen that I was telling you about," Holly said. "I told her how you've been helping me connect with my—*feminine instincts.*"

"Um, yes," I stammered, unsure how much Holly had shared with her roommate. "We've been exploring some mutual interests."

"That's not the *only* thing she's been exploring," Jen said, leaning over to give Holly a long passionate kiss on her lips.

"I'm glad to see you two have finally connected," I said. "It sounded as if Holly might never break you away from your boyfriend, Jen."

"He wasn't really my boyfriend. More of a *boy-toy* to mess around with occasionally. I've had my eye on Holly ever since we became roommates. If it wasn't for you, I might never have known she was also interested in girls."

"Not just *any* girl," Holly said, reaching out her hand to intertwine her fingers with Jen's. "Only you."

"And *Jade* apparently," Jen said, nodding toward the screen.

"We found each other by accident," I interjected, not wanting to create a barrier between the two lovers. "Holly was just trying to find an outlet for her emerging feelings, to see if they were real."

"I can see why," Jen said, leaning toward the screen. "You're just as pretty and sexy as Holly said. I think she needed a more experienced lover to help her find her path."

"Not to mention how to learn how to make love to another woman," Holly winked at me.

"Yes," Jen said, tilting an eyebrow. "She's been trying out some of her new moves on me. I should thank you for your mentoring. It might have taken us *months* to figure out all the special things we girls can do with one another."

My pussy fluttered at the thought of the two girls making out all night long.

"Oh? You've been practicing?" I teased, fishing for more details.

Jen suddenly lifted herself up and straddled Holly's hips, facing away from the camera.

"To say the least," she said. "Would you like to see? Maybe you can show us a few new moves."

I squirmed on my bed, suddenly aware of the wet spot forming in the seat of my robe.

"I'd love to watch you ravish each other. Do you mind if this old lady has a little fun while you two go at it?"

"We were kind of hoping you would," Jen said. "And you're far from an old lady. Can we see a bit more of your body? Holly said you have an amazing figure."

"Absolutely," I said, scarcely believing my luck having the opportunity to have online sex with two gorgeous young co-eds. I quickly tore off my robe and pulled down my panties, feeling the torrent of fluid between my legs soaking into my bedsheets.

"Can we see your tits, too?" Jen said. "Those are some pretty fine looking hooters."

I hesitated for a moment revealing any more of my body, out of concern this was shaping up to be a one-sided show, rather than the two-way exchange I'd enjoyed with Holly so far. It was obvious that Jen was the more aggressive partner in their relationship, and I didn't want Holly feeling embarrassed or left out.

"Am I the *only* one getting undressed?" I asked.

"No way," Holly said, pulling her T-shirt over her head. Jen quickly followed suit, and the two girls pressed their bare breasts together while they kissed passionately.

As I watched the girls rubbing their bodies together, I pulled my camisole over my head and began pinching my nipples. Jen pressed her body forward, tilting Holly down onto the bed, then they twisted their bodies so they could watch the screen from the side.

"Damn, Jade," Jen said. "Holly wasn't kidding. You have a gorgeous body. I can see how she got off so easily watching you."

"I can't hold a candle to you guys," I said, admiring the two girls' smooth, flexible bodies. "I wish everything stood as firm and perky on me as it does on you. You've got a very sexy body too, Jen."

"Talk dirty to us," she said. "Tell us what you want us to do. Holly was telling me about some of the things you like."

I guess all pretenses are off at this point, I thought. *It's time to get down and dirty.* I spread my legs and placed my fingers over my slick opening.

"I want to watch you suck on Holly's pretty nipples. Make them hard and long again, like I saw them yesterday."

Jen leaned forward and took Holly's left breast into her mouth, then turned her head to glance into the camera. I pushed my laptop away from me a few inches so they could see my pussy and hips displayed in front of the screen. As I circled my clit with the tip of my fingers, I squeezed my breast with my other hand and moaned at the sight of Holly's teat in her roommate's mouth.

"Mmm," Jen hummed, as she tickled and teased Holly's tips.

"You are one sexy momma," Jen said, popping her mouth off Holly's nipple with a smack. "No wonder I caught her coming when I walked in the door yesterday. You could put any girl over the edge with a body like that."

"Happy to oblige anytime," I panted, feeling my juices running down my thighs.

"We might have to arrange that," Jen said, smiling at the camera. "But right now, I just want to fuck my girl while you get off watching us. What would you like us to do now?"

I couldn't believe they were letting me direct the action like some kind of erotic movie director. I moved my laptop a little closer toward my body and leaned closer to the screen.

"I want to watch you *taste* her," I said. "I want to watch Holly twisting all over your face while you make her cum with your tongue."

"My pleasure," Jen said. "She *does* taste so sweet. I can't get enough of her sex in my mouth."

As Jen slithered down Holly's body toward her hips, Holly turned the laptop with her hand to allow me to take in all the action.

"You're so sexy, Jade," she purred as Jen placed her head between her legs. "Thanks for joining us tonight. I wanted to share this with you."

"*I'm* the lucky one," I said. "I'm just glad you finally connected with Jen. It's so great to see you together this way."

"You have no idea," Jen said, placing her hands beside Holly's hips and pulling her toward her. Holly gasped and arched her back when Jen's lips found her pearl.

"Yes, Jen," she panted. "Suck me right there. Lick my clit while Jade watches us.

When I saw the look on Holly's face from Jen's touch, I buried my fingers in my pussy and began rubbing my clit with the palm of my hand. By now I was soaking wet, and a huge stain had begun to spread over my sheets between my legs.

"Yes—finger your pussy," Holly moaned as she watched me jilling myself. Jen turned her face to see what I was doing then began lapping her tongue up and down Holly's slit.

"Suck me Jen," Holly moaned. "Make me cum all over your face."

"Fuck, Holly," I groaned, watching my fantasy come true. "That is so hot! You're going to make me cum soon too."

"Cum with me, Jade," Holly said. "Let me watch you squirt while I cum in Jen's mouth. I'm close—"

"Oh God," I suddenly hissed, clamping down on my fingers. As the insides of my pussy began contracting in a powerful orgasm, I pulled my fingers out of my hole and began spraying all over the computer screen. I was so lost in the throes of pleasure, I didn't care that I might be ruining my computer. Right now, I just wanted to show Holly the effect she was having on me.

"Holy fuck, Jade," Holly groaned. "I'm cumming! Spray your juices all over me!"

Holly lifted her hips off the mattress then slammed her body back down onto the bed as she grabbed the back of Jen's head. She pulled her tightly against her pussy while she jerked and thrashed on the sheets. Jen glanced out the corner of her eye toward their computer as her eyes widened watching me gush all over my camera. My image must have been blurry from the juices running over the lens, but this just seemed to get Holly even more excited.

"God, how I'd love you feel you cumming on me like that," she panted, slowly coming down from her long and intense orgasm. When her thighs finally stopped quaking, Jen lifted her head and smiled toward the camera.

"You are one hot momma, Jade," she said, wiping the back of her hand over her lips to clear some of Holly's juices off her face. "I can see why Holly wanted to see you again. This is even *more* fun with a sexy spectator."

"Sorry," I said, lifting my camisole off the bed to wipe my screen and keyboard. "I made quite a mess."

"Are you kidding me?" Jen said. "That might be the sexiest thing I've ever seen. I never even knew a woman could squirt like that."

"Only when I'm really worked up," I said. "I guess I lubricate a bit more than some women. When I come really hard, my muscles just push it out of me. I got pretty turned on watching Holly cum on your face."

"You weren't the only ones getting turned on by that," Jen said. "I'm about to burst at the seams myself."

I smiled at Jen and raised my finger to request a short break.

"Can you give me just one minute to clean up this mess before we continue? I'm afraid all this fluid might get inside my computer and short it or something. The last thing I need right now is to lose the ability to see both of you getting off together. I'll be right back."

4

—————

JOINING FORCES

I got up and scurried to the bathroom and ran some water over a facecloth, then wrung it out and came back to the bed. I wiped the screen, camera, and keyboard with the wet cloth, then dried all the surfaces with another dry cloth. When I peered back at the screen, I saw that Holly and Jen were lying sideways on the bed, kissing one another.

"Can you guys see me clearly?" I said, hesitating to interrupt up their embrace.

They turned toward their screen and nodded.

"Perfect," Jen said. "What would you like to see us do now? Hopefully something with a little *together* action."

"Definitely," I said. "I think it's time you got some direct stimulation too, Jen." It was obvious to me that Jen was the dominant one, and I was eager to watch her fuck Holly. "Can you get on top of Holly and place your hips over hers so you're scissoring your pussies together?"

She raised herself up and straddled Holly's hips diagonally, with one knee on the outside of her hips and the other one resting just inside her thighs.

"You mean like this?" Jen said.

"Yes. Now lift Holly's right leg up so you can get more direct contact between your vulvas."

Holly lifted her leg straight up in the air then Jen placed it over her right shoulder, twisting Holly's hips sideways. Now the two girls were locked in a tight scissor position, with their pussies tightly clamped together.

"Mmm, that feels good, Jen," Holly purred.

"We haven't tried it *this* way yet," Jen nodded. "You're quite a sex coach, Jade. We'll have to do this more often."

"Any place, any time," I smiled. "But I think you two can take it from here. You're in charge now, Jen. You should be able to get plenty of direct stimulation this way."

As Jen began to swing her hips forward and back against Holly's pussy, she let out a low moan.

"Fuck, yes," she purred. "I can feel your clit rubbing against mine, Holly."

"Fuck me, Jen," Holly panted. "Fuck my cunt with your sweet pussy."

"Damn straight I will," Jen said, pulling Holly's raised leg tightly between her tits, increasing the speed of her hip movement between Holly's flared legs.

As the two girls began humping each other, I mimicked Jen's position by lifting myself up and kneeling on my bed. Then I reached over to my side table and pulled out a dome-shaped silicone cushion with a vulva impression carved in the top. I positioned the device between my legs, then I lowered myself onto it and began grinding my pussy into the artificial vulva.

"Damn, girl," Jen panted. "You've got all the toys. What *is* that thing?"

"It's just a little something I use on lonely nights to imagine I'm doing what you're doing right now to Holly. Sometimes I like to fantasize that I'm tribbing another woman instead of just using my hands or a vibrator."

"That's pretty hot," Jen moaned. "Are you fantasizing about rubbing *us* that way right now?"

"Definitely," I panted, spreading my legs wider and pressing myself harder against the cushion.

"Does that thing *vibrate* by any chance?" Holly said, winking at me.

"It does, as a matter of fact."

"Show me."

I flicked a switch on the side of the cushion, and the vulva began vibrating between my legs.

"Uhnn," I groaned, throwing my head back in pleasure.

"Yes, Jade," Holly panted as she watched me. "Fuck her like you'd fuck me. I want to watch you cum all over my pussy like you did on the screen a few minutes ago."

"I think that can be arranged," I smiled, feeling my wetness spreading over the cushion.

"God, that's hot," Jen panted, watching me fuck my artificial lover on the screen. "My pussy's on fire, Holl. I'm going to cum for you soon."

"I feel you, Jen," Holly moaned. "Caress me with your sweet lips. Spread your love all over me."

Jen wrapped her arms tightly around Holly's upturned leg and suddenly began convulsing against her hips.

"It's happening, Holl! I'm cumming! Your pussy feels so good against mine."

"I'm cumming with you, Jen!" Holly grunted. "Press your pussy against me. Feel me cumming inside you."

As I watched the two girls twisting their bodies in simultaneous orgasm, I lost all control and began spurting all over my domed lover. While the girls thrashed their bodies together, we watched each other as we screamed in one powerful, collective climax. After what seemed like an eternity at the peak of pleasure, we all collapsed onto our respective beds, panting as we peered into our screens.

"You guys seemed to enjoy that," I said. "I told you there's lots of different ways we girls can have fun, Holly."

"You weren't kidding," Holly said, trying to catch her breath.

"The possibilities become endless with such an interesting collection of toys," Jen said. "What *other* interesting devices have you got to share with us?"

I leaned over and reached into my nightstand and pulled another toy out of the drawer, being careful to hide it from their view.

"I've already shown Holly how to use my special rabbit vibrator," I said. "But my real favorite is one *two* women can enjoy at the same time."

I held up the twelve-inch-long two-sided silicone phallus and bent it playfully between my two hands.

"Scissoring is even more fun when you've got something filling you up inside."

"Holy fuck!" Jen exclaimed, with wide eyes. "That think is huge! How do you fit that inside you? I could never—"

"You don't. It's meant to be shared with your lover. Each of you takes a separate end while you fuck each other, kind of like a man. There's nothing quite like it."

"I can imagine," Jen said. "I wish we had one of those things to play with right now."

"Well, *actually*—" Holly said, reaching over her head to remove something from underneath her pillow. She held a big purple dildo up in the air and waved it sexily from side to side. "I took the liberty today when you went out for a while to get one myself. After Jade explained how these things could be used, I thought you might like to give it a try..."

"*Hell* yes!" Jen said, raising herself back onto her knees excitedly. "Show me how to use it, Holly. Maybe Jade can play along with us on her end at the same time."

"It'll be my pleasure," I said, feeling another rivulet of juices running down the inside of my thighs. "I just wish we had a *three-sided* version so we could all do it together for real."

"I didn't see one of those at the sex shop," Holly said.

"Don't worry about me. I'll improvise. I'm just happy to watch you two enjoying yourselves. Now let me see you join together using that big snake."

"Lie down on the bed," Holly instructed to Jen. "This time it's my turn to fuck you."

Jen lay down with her hips about a foot away from Holly's, while Holly inserted one end of the long dildo into her pussy. Then she pushed closer to Jen and placed the other end at her opening. As they pressed their hips together, the giant dildo slowly disappeared into Jen's cavity as she uttered a low guttural moan.

"Yes—just like that," I purred, watching the two girls begin to hump their hips together.

"What about you?" Holly said, tilting her head back toward the camera. "What are you going to do while we're having all the fun?"

"I need something moving inside me too," I said.

I reached back into my nightstand and pulled out my rabbit vibrator and leaned back against my headboard. It made a loud slurping sound as I inserted it inside me.

"Sounds like *somebody's* still wet," Holly smiled.

"It looks that way. I hope you won't be distracted if I make a little noise while you two fuck each other."

"Not at all," Jen said, pressing her pussy closer to Holly's. "We intend to make some rude sounds of our own."

"Mmm," Holly moaned. "I like the feeling of you moving inside me, Jen. Fuck me with your big cock."

"This is way better than a real cock," Jen purred, smiling at Holly. "It's double the pleasure. I can fuck my partner at the same time I'm getting filled up by her. Who needs a man when you've got so many fun ways to play with a girl?"

"Exactly," I said. "I told you there was no going back once you experienced real lesbian loving, Holly."

"I'm *never* going back," Holly moaned as Jen picked up the pace of her hip movements. "Everything I need is right here on this bed with me."

"Normally I'd agree," Jen panted, watching the fluttering rabbit ears of my vibrator rubbing up against my clit. "But I think Jade has a slight advantage with that dual-purpose vibrator. How can we get direct clitoral stimulation like you in this position?"

"No one said you can't *touch* yourselves," I said. "Half the fun of using a double-sided dildo with your partner is watching them stimulate themselves while you fuck each other. Go ahead and rub your clits with your hands."

The two girls slid their right hand over each of their mounds, then reached down their other side and clasped hands.

"That's the idea," I said. "Does that feel better?"

"Better," Jen panted, as the girls pulled themselves closer together with their interlocking hands.

As I watched them twist and roll their bodies together, I leaned forward and kneeled on the bed. I placed my rabbit vibrator underneath me then I lowered my hips, letting the pressure of the mattress insert it inside me.

"You guys look so hot together," I moaned. "Now I'm thinking about that three-sided dildo again. I'm going to have to see if I can find one of those."

"If you do, you'll have to let us know," Holly groaned, watching me hump my dildo. "I'd love to try a three-way for real someday."

"What about you, Jen?" I said. "Would you be up for that too?"

"Fuck, yes," she purred. "I'd love to squeeze those big melons of yours while we all fuck each other silly."

"I'll look into it," I said. "Right now, I want to imagine I'm there with you girls. Can you see me? I'm imagining myself fucking you both over top."

"Yes," Holly panted. "Fuck us, Jade. Press your wet pussy against our hips and gush all over our stomachs. I want to see you cum again."

"Fuck," I moaned, imagining the movement of the animated vibrator inside me as if it were two girls underneath me creating the action. "I can't hold it much longer. I'm going to cum all over both of you soon!"

The two girls clasped their hands together on both sides and pulled themselves together. As they gnashed their clits together, the dildo disappeared completely inside their pussies.

"Oh God, Holly," Jen grunted. "I'm going to cum too. Are you almost there?"

"Yes, Jen," Holly moaned, twisting her head to watch me jackrabbiting on the vibrator deeply embedded in my pussy. "Cum Jade!"

As the two girls began to pull their torsos off the mattress and look at each other with wild eyes, I felt the first wave of passion roll over me.

"It's happening!" I shouted, holding the base of my vibrator with two hands. "Cum for me, Holly!"

The two girls' mouths gaped opened in a wide yaw, then they screamed out loud as their bodies writhed against one another in mutual ecstasy.

"Fuckk," Jen growled. "I feel you, Holly! I feel you cumming against me. Cum for me baby!"

"Yes Jen!" Holly screamed as her whole body quaked in an intense orgasm, her pointy tits shaking like two trembling pyramids over her quivering tummy while the girls held each other with tensed outstretched arms.

As each of us quivered and moaned over our embedded phalluses, I couldn't stop fantasizing about what it would be like to merge together in a true ménage à trois.

If they don't have a three-sided dildo, I'll have to make one for myself, I thought, peering down at the giant puddle between my legs.

VOLUME TWO

THE SPA

VICTORIA RUSH

1

"What's up, girl?" my best friend Hannah said to me at our weekly lunch date. "You look a little run down. Have you been taking care of yourself?"

"I've been going to yoga class as often as I can, and I think I'm eating reasonably well. But I've kind of been flitting from one empty relationship to another, and I guess I'm in a bit of a rut."

"Mmm," Hannah nodded. "Maybe you need to break away from your routine for a change. You know, mix up the scenery, go somewhere you can relax and recharge your batteries."

"What did you have in mind?" I said.

"I've been thinking," she smiled with a slight curl of her lip. "I've heard about this new spa in town that takes a different slant on the whole wellness concept."

"How so?"

"Well, for one thing, it's for ladies only."

"That's nothing new. Ninety-five percent of the clientele at most spas is already women."

"This one's on the top floor of one of the tallest skyscrapers in Chicago. It's got a retractable roof and a beautiful open-air patio surrounding a huge pool with magnificent views of the city and the lake."

"That *does* sound a little more upscale than most," I nodded. "But if that's its big claim to fame, I'm not sure that's going to be enough to pull me out of my funk."

"What if I told you it's a *naked* spa?"

"What do you mean?" I said, suddenly intrigued. "You mean customers receive facials and massages in the nude?"

"Well yes, but it's much more than that. I mean *everybody's* naked, including in the common areas like the pool, sauna, and exercise studio."

"Really? Like a nudist camp or something?"

"A very *elite* nudist camp," she smiled. "With all the spa amenities. Where everybody is super wellness-oriented and in fabulous shape. Imagine sitting poolside watching all the hot women going in and out of the pool and cavorting in the hot tub."

I shifted unsteadily on my chair, suddenly realizing how wet my panties had become envisioning the scenario.

"Is there a *lot* of cavorting going on?"

"Let's just say it's a voyeur's paradise, where women are encouraged to mingle. From what I've heard, it's Chicago's answer to Plato's Retreat. There's allegedly a ton of extra-curricular activities going on. Don't tell me that doesn't get your juices going."

"Um–*yeah*," I said, feeling my pussy throb at the idea of an all-girls venue. "That does sound a little different. What about the staff? They don't have a problem with all that lewd socializing?"

"Quite the opposite. Apparently, they're just as involved in the delivery of the special services. Can you imagine getting a full-body massage with a hot masseuse with all the extra benefits? Or a Brazilian, or a pedicure, or a facial where they make sure you're satisfied in *every* possible way?"

I leaned back in my chair, scrunching up my face.

"Don't you think it would be kind of weird getting a wax where the aesthetician is focused on more than just cleaning things up down there?"

"You never know until you try," Hannah said. "Come on, Jade–you deserve to be pampered for a change. This is a place you can go where there's no judging, no expectations, no relationship pressures. You can indulge as little or as much as you wish in the carnal opportunities. Or just lie in the sun, go for a dip in the pool, and take in the scenery."

"The very *erotic* scenery," I smiled.

"That never stopped you before," she said, arching an eyebrow.

"Okay," I said. "You've twisted my arm. When did you have in mind for this little excursion?"

"Tomorrow at noon," she said, holding up two tickets. "I've already paid for both of us. My treat."

"Are you planning to be my wingwoman to keep me out of trouble?"

"Fuck *that*," Hannah chuckled. "I'm going to be your *partner-in-crime*, to make sure you get into as much trouble as possible."

2

———————

The following day, I met Hannah in the lobby of an office tower on Magnificent Mile. It was a beautiful sunny day, and I could see all the way down Grand Avenue toward the Navy Pier and Lake Michigan. I was ready to forget my troubles and lose myself in the luxury and decadence of the upscale spa. I had no idea what I was in for, but the throbbing in my pussy suggested it would be anything but boring.

"So, are you ready for this?" Hannah said while we waited for the elevator on the ground floor.

"I think so," I said. "My *mind* isn't so sure, but my body seems to have other ideas."

We stepped into the lift and Hannah nodded, tapping the button for the sixty-third floor.

"I'm just as excited as you are to see what this is all about. My mind's been racing with all the possibilities ever since I bought the tickets."

"You had this planned for me all along, didn't you?" I said.

"Of course," Hannah smirked. "How could I not invite my bestie to the hottest show in town?"

When the elevator reached the top floor and the doors opened, I saw a pretty attendant dressed in a blue uniform sitting behind a frosted-glass desk flanked by a streaming water wall.

"It's impressive looking, that's for sure," I said. "But I thought you said all the staff were naked?"

"They have to present a professional face to the general public," Hannah said. "But I assure you, once we get behind the reception area, it will be an entirely different picture. Come on, let's check this place out."

We strolled up to the front counter, and the attendant looked up from her computer screen.

"Good afternoon," the girl said. "How can I be of service?"

"We have two day-passes," Hannah said, sliding the tickets over the counter.

"Of course," the girl said, peering at the tickets. "You're welcome to use all of our club's features at your leisure. There's the pool of course, the outdoor patio, the hot tub, sauna, and exercise studio. But if you wish to avail yourselves of the special services, you'll have to make an appointment."

"What services do you offer, specifically?"

"Our aestheticians and massage therapists provide facials, mani-cures/pedicures, massages, and intimate grooming."

Hannah turned toward me and smiled.

"What do you think, Jade? What would you like to do first?"

"I think I'm pretty good with the grooming. How about a massage?"

I looked toward the attendant.

"Do you offer doubles massages? When's your next opening?"

"We do," she said. "Our therapists are just finishing up with another appointment. They should be available in about twenty minutes if you'd both like to give it a try."

"Yes, thank you," Hannah nodded.

The attendant handed each of us a card key to enter the premises and separate locker keys.

"The change room is through the door to the left. Each of the service areas is clearly marked. The massage therapists will be waiting for you at one p.m."

"Is there a particular dress code while traveling about the common areas?" Hannah asked.

"You'll find a terrycloth robe in each of your lockers and two large bath towels. You're welcome to wear either of these in the common areas or nothing at all, if you prefer. We want you to feel as relaxed and comfortable as possible at all times. Most of our guests choose to relax in the nude, as they find that most liberating."

Liberating, indeed, I smiled at the attendant, noticing a gleam in her eye.

Hannah and I took our keys and passed through the locked guest door, then followed the signs to the change room. When we got there, there was a handful of women coming in and out of the showers, making little effort to conceal their naked bodies. Most of them looked to be in their twenties and early thirties, with well-toned figures and golden-brown skin.

"Looks like we're going be the old ladies of the bunch," Hannah chuckled, opening her locker next to mine.

"I'm okay with that," I said, taking off my clothes and hanging them in the locker next to the robe. "If this is any indication of what the rest of the customers look like, that'll work for me. Besides, we're no slouches. I think we can hold our own against the competition."

Hannah peered at a pretty blonde giving her the eye as she bent over to step out of her pants.

"Something tells me there's going to be a *lot* of holding our own against these ladies before the day is over," she winked.

I glanced at a slim African-American girl emerging from one of the showers. She had flawless caramel-colored skin and a model-perfect figure with firm, high breasts, a narrow waist, and an exquis-itely rounded ass. As she patted her short afro dry, I stole a glance between her legs, watching the water drip down over her bald, brown mound.

"Jesus," I said. "I could jump any one of these girls right now. I hope these ladies are just getting *started* their spa treatment, not finishing."

"Not to worry," Hannah smiled, noticing me drooling at the pretty black girl. "I'm pretty sure there's lots more where those came from. Just try to keep your dick in your pants for a little longer while we ease our way into this experience."

"Whatever you say, boss," I said. "So what's the protocol? Do we wear our robes into the massage room or traipse around in the buff like everyone else it seems to be doing?"

"I don't see any harm in wearing the robe to start," Hannah said. "Besides, we need *somewhere* we store our locker keys."

"Come on," she said, glancing at her phone screen before placing it on the locker shelf and locking the door. "It's time for our massage."

I followed Hannah down the hall to the waiting area for the massages, where we sat in the plush chairs, picking up two copies of Vogue magazine lying on the adjacent tables. As I began leafing through the glamour shots of the gorgeous models, I wondered how many of them had frequented this place. The African-American girl I saw in the change room certainly could have qualified for any of these shoots, and I felt my nipples hardening at the idea of engaging with her later. After a few minutes, the door to the massage room opened and a nude brunette girl approached us.

She had a more athletic figure than the black girl from the locker room, but was equally stunning. With large, round tits and a perfectly toned stomach and bare midriff, my pussy began watering just looking at her.

"Are you Hannah and Jade for the one o'clock massage appointment?"

"Um, yes," I stammered, momentarily taken aback by her casual attitude and Amazonesque figure.

"Please," she said. "Come in."

When we entered the room, I saw a second attendant leaning over a sink washing her hands as her tight ass flexed over rippling hamstrings and calves. I looked at Hannah with wide eyes, mouthing the words *Holy Shit!* She peered back at me with an equally incredulous look, shrugging her shoulders.

"Just go with the flow, baby," she whispered.

In the middle of the room rested two side-by-side massage tables about four feet apart, covered with a long bath sheet and a rolled-up towel resting in the middle section.

"Can we hang your robes for you?" the brunette said as the blonde attendant turned around, drying her hands.

She was even more beautiful than the brunette, with long silky hair tied up in a bun and a slender figure with the most exquisite tits I'd seen in a long time. With her compact round ass, long slender legs, and mouth-wateringly curvy hips, she had the figure of a twenty-year-old stripper. I could feel the moisture rapidly building up between my legs as a trickle of lubrication dripped down the inside of my thigh.

"By all means," Hannah said, practically throwing her robe at the attendant.

"Make yourselves comfortable on the massage tables, facing face-down," the brunette said, obviously the more experienced of the two girls.

When I lay down on one of the benches, I was happy when I saw the blonde girl approach my table with a bottle of massage oil. I would have been happy to have either girl touch me, but there was something about the blonde one that got my juices flowing. As I watched the brunette hovering over Hannah's naked body pouring oil into her hands, I glanced at Hannah with wide eyes. Neither of us had to say a word, since both of us were thinking the same thing. This was as close to heaven as two living and breathing people surely could have gotten.

When I felt the blonde's slippery hands run up my spine starting from the small of my back, at first I flinched from the unexpected sensation. But after she began softly pressing her thumbs and fingers into my muscles, I slowly relaxed, flitting my eyes in sublime bliss. Normally, I closed my eyes when I got a massage, concentrating on the relaxing feeling of my masseuse's fingers kneading my body. But with Hannah lying right next to me being serviced by a gorgeous Amazon, I kept them wide open, following her every movement and muscle twitch.

As she pressed her fingers into Hannah's back and slid her hands up and down her spine, I watched her tits jiggling and the muscles in her arms and stomach flexing. Her lower body was partially obscured by Hannah's prone figure, but that didn't stop me from dreaming about slipping my fingers into her bare snatch and licking her like a puppy dog. When the girls moved around to opposite sides of our tables revealing their bare asses for both of us to see, Hannah and I looked at one another again with wide eyes.

As I watched the front of my masseuse's body tensing and flexing only inches away from me, it took every ounce of my willpower not to reach out from the side of my table and touch her bald pussy. The more she caressed me, the more worked up I got watching the two girls' asses wiggling mere inches apart, and my hips began to squirm atop the rolled towel pressing into my pubis.

Just when I thought I couldn't take it any longer, the two masseuses moved to the other end of our bodies and began pressing their fingers into our calves, slowly working their way up our legs along the insides of our thighs. When the blonde girl reached the base of my buttocks, she stopped just short of my dripping slit then rolled her hands over my buttocks, squeezing them firmly. I pressed my mound down hard on the bumpy towel, desperately trying to give my aching clit some direct friction.

Feeling my buttocks flexing in her hands and sensing my rising tension, she swept her hands around the sides of my ass, cupping my cheeks with her thumbs pointed toward my fluttering pussy. I spread my legs further apart, inviting her to move her hand closer, and I gasped when she began running her thumbs up and down the sides of my slippery folds.

God yes, I thought, feeling my heart beginning to pound in my chest. *That's where I need your touch right now.*

I glanced over at Hannah, who had an equally intense look on her face as her attendant leaned over, caressing her vulva. I could see the slit of her masseuse's pussy between her round globes, and my eyes darted back and forth between the view of the blonde's bare mound moving inches away from my face and the brunette's inviting pussy glistening in the bright light of the massage room on the other side of Hannah's table.

I peered over at Hannah with my mouth agape and whispered *Thank You*. She simply smiled back at me and nodded knowingly. Something told me she knew exactly what she'd gotten us into, but at this precise moment I couldn't care less about her devious plan. Suddenly, the blonde girl adjusted her position with her left hand rested atop the base of my spine, while her other hand curled under my cheeks, penetrating my hole. When I felt her fingers enter my tunnel, I groaned, tilting my ass higher in the air.

Now I knew what the rolled-up towel was intended for. It was obviously meant to give the masseuses easier access to our undercarriage for this express purpose. As I began to roll my hips in concert with the blonde's probing of my pussy, I felt a stream of oil drip onto my buttocks, flowing down the crack of my ass over my rosebud and her dripping hand, now firmly embedded in my cunt. When I felt her other hand slide down over my ass and begin to massage my pucker, I groaned loudly and closed my eyes.

I was no longer interested in seeing what the other girl was doing to Hannah. I just wanted to concentrate on the heavenly sensation being administered by my own masseuse. When she began flicking my clit with the two little fingers of her right hand while she stimulated the walls of my pussy with her other fingers, I couldn't contain my pleasure any longer.

"Oh God," I moaned, fucking her hands with my ass and my pussy. My entire perineum from my asshole down to my clit was being simultaneously stimulated by the most sexy woman I'd seen in a long time.

"Yes," I purred, opening my eyes to see Hannah equally glazed over as her masseuse ministered to her in a similar manner.

I wondered if the couples' massage was designed to provide each of us simultaneous attention so we could arc through our pleasure in tandem. But at this point I hardly cared, as I surrendered to the mounting pleasure building inside me. Hannah and I peered at each other's faces while we read our bodies, knowing exactly what was happening to each other as we watched our reactions. We raised our arms over our heads and gripped the top of our padded tables tightly with our hands, and our mouths began to gape open as a flush rolled over each of our cheeks.

"Oh fuck," I groaned, feeling my orgasm beginning to pulse through me as my whole body began to shake. As I began clamping down on the blonde's fingers inside my pussy, she slipped her oiled thumb into my pucker while she fucked both of my holes as I writhed in delirious pleasure on the massage table.

"Uhnnn," Hannah groaned as I watched her ass quivering in the throes of her own powerful climax. The sight of the two gorgeous masseuse's fucking us with both hands while their bodies tensed and writhed overtop of our prone bodies was the most erotic thing I'd experienced in ages.

Hannah and I trembled and moaned on the massage tables for what seemed like an eternity, then our bodies both fell limp as our climaxes receded. For the first time in a long time, I felt completely relaxed and satisfied.

Maybe this spa idea wasn't such a bad idea after all, I smiled toward Hannah lying on the table next to me.

3

____

After Hannah and I recovered from our dual massages, we headed to the pool to relax. The view of the city from the rooftop patio was magnificent, but the view *inside* was even more heart-stopping. Scores of naked women paraded in and out of the pool, while another group giggled inside an oversize, bubbling Jacuzzi. With the glass roof retracted, the bright overhead sun reflected off their glistening skin like sequins on their bare bodies.

We found two lounge chairs facing the shallow end of the pool and lay our bath towels on the padded cushions, then propped up the seatbacks so we'd have a good view of the action. The shallow end had descending steps leading into the basin, so we had a front-row seat for viewing the women as they slunk in and out of the water. As I watched the procession of beauties emerging from the pool dripping in erotic sensuality, I squeezed my thighs together trying to quiet my burning clit.

"You weren't kidding about this place being a voyeur's paradise," I chuckled to Hannah.

"Tell me about it," she said. "I can't decide if I prefer them coming or going."

"I could come again watching them either way. Is *everybody* in this place drop-dead gorgeous with model-perfect figures?"

"Well, it *is* the city's most exclusive spa, so I guess these girls know how to take care of themselves. But I also suspect a lot of it has to do with the fact that they know they're going to be under a microscope traipsing around in the nude. Maybe only the prettiest ones feel confident enough to flaunt their bodies so openly."

"Don't get me wrong," I said. "I'm definitely enjoying the show. It's just that I haven't felt this self-conscious about my body in a long time."

Hannah cocked her head toward me, peering over the top of her sunglasses.

"Don't sell yourself short, girl. You're just as pretty and sexy as any one of these hot mamas. Maybe you should get out there and do a little flaunting of your own."

"Perhaps in a little while," I said. "Right now, I'm just happy to do the watching."

"So are you glad I twisted your arm to come up here?" she said, lying back in her chair to soak up the sun.

"Definitely. This is even more dreamy than I imagined."

"And did you enjoy your massage?"

"Couldn't you tell? I think my masseuse probed every one of my erogenous zones."

"That's what I call a *full-body* massage," Hannah smiled.

"I was kind of hoping they'd flip us over afterward and get on top of us to complete the procedure. I don't know about you, but I had a hard time resisting the temptation to reach out and grope them as they moved around the table."

"I suspect that was all by design," Hannah nodded. "To build up our excitement for the big finish."

"That was a hell of a happy ending. I haven't come that hard in months."

"And we're just getting started," Hannah smiled. "Think of all the opportunities to connect in this place."

Suddenly, I noticed the pretty black girl from the locker room emerge from the outside patio and begin to walk in our direction.

"Oh, I'm *thinking*, alright," I said, pushing myself higher in my chair to get a better view.

Hannah followed my line of sight toward the girl and smiled.

"Isn't that the same girl you were eyeballing in the change room? She seems to be just as interested in you as you were in her."

As she moved closer toward us, we made eye contact, checking each other's figures out.

"I dunno, Han," I said. "I think she's out of my league. She looks like an African goddess."

"Well it appears that she's going to give us a bird's-eye view of her figure at least. Maybe she'll take a dip in the pool, where we can get a closer look at her."

As the girl walked toward the shallow end of the pool, I watched her tits jiggling on her chest and her long leg muscles flexing. When she got within a few feet of us, she turned toward the turquoise water and paused at the top of the steps. Her backside was even more spectacular than her front, with her swelling hips and a perfectly round ass accentuating her tawny, hourglass figure.

"Fuck me," I whispered to Hannah, peering down the crack of her ass toward the dark folds showing between her slightly parted thighs.

"That could be arranged if you play your cards right," she chuckled.

After a few seconds, the girl stepped into the water, slowly immersing her body into the sparkling surf. Then she leaned forward and began swimming toward the other end using a graceful breast stroke. As her legs flapped in and out, I watched her sexy ass rising and falling under the surface while the water swirled over her caramel body.

"Oh my God," I panted. "*Pinch* me to make sure I'm not dreaming."

"It's not a dream, babe," Hannah smiled. "That is one sexy-ass, flesh-and-blood woman."

"Just when I thought it couldn't possibly get any hotter than those two masseuses that worked us over. I'd take *this* one over three of them in a heartbeat."

When the girl reached the other end of the pool, she flipped over onto her other side and began swimming with a backstroke toward us. While her arms slowly windmilled through the water, her body rolled from side to side as the water washed over her sensuous breasts like waves on a beach. The closer she got to me, the more my heart raced, imagining her swimming right into my moistening lap.

"Yes, sweetheart," I purred, spreading my legs apart. "Dock yourself right here."

Hannah and I sat mesmerized watching her sylphlike figure slicing through the water, until one of her hands tapped the steps in the shallow end. Then she turned around and walked out of the water directly in front of us, smiling as she made eye contact with me. I couldn't help running my eyes over the front of her dripping body as my legs twitched involuntarily. Then she turned and retraced her steps around the perimeter of the pool, reclining in a vacant lounge chair at the opposite end.

"Did you see how she looked at you?" Hannah said, peering over at me. "She was practically fucking you with her eyes."

"I hardly noticed, watching the rest of her incredible body."

"I think you need to take advantage of this opportunity while the iron is still hot," she said. "Why don't you go over there and introduce yourself?"

"I wouldn't exactly say that was a green light to go hit on her. I don't want to intrude on her privacy if she just wants some peace and quiet."

"Well then, why don't you give her some of her own medicine by parading your body up and down the pool for everyone else to see? Let's see if she takes the bait."

"I don't know if *bait* is the right metaphor in this case, but I'd be thrilled if she gobbled me up right about now. I could use a refreshing dip in the pool anyways. After that hot massage session and watching that nymph take a sexy bath, I need to cool off. Hold my chair for me?"

"I wouldn't dream of giving it away. You go girl, go get your Lorelei."

I raised myself up from my chair then walked up to the edge of the shallow end and paused, peering across the reflecting surface hoping to catch the girl watching me from the other end of the pool. Although I was a little more full-figured than her, I maintained a tight, yoga-toned physique, with full, perky breasts, a flat stomach, and curvy hips. My pussy throbbed at the thought of her ogling me as I had with her.

While I lowered myself into the water, I kept my gaze pointed down, pretending to ignore her. Mimicking her lead, I began swimming breast strokes in her direction, with my head bobbing in and out of the water. When I neared the far wall, I glanced up at her chair resting near the edge of the pool and noticed her legs were slightly parted and she had a sexy smile on her face.

Jesus, I thought, touching the wall right in front of her. *Was she signaling her interest in me the same way I had earlier?*

As I turned around, I couldn't help smiling at our sexy cat-and-mouse game, then I pushed back from the wall floating on my back, using a reverse breast stroke technique. While I flapped my legs slowly in and out, I lifted my ass to the surface of the water, letting her watch the churning surf rising and falling over my exposed bare pussy. As I swung my arms slowly behind me, I glanced at the side of the pool and noticed that all the women were staring at my breasts poking out of the water.

Good, I thought. *Maybe if the African-American girl sees that I'm attracting the attention of some of the other pretty women, she'll make the next move.*

When I reached the shallow end, I walked up the stairs slowly so the girl on the other end could watch my round ass dripping with moisture. Then I lay down on my lounge chair next to Hannah, not even bothering to dry off.

"Holy shit, girl," she said. "I think you might have just one-upped your African goddess. Every set of eyes in the room was watching you as you swam across both lengths of the pool. You even got *me* going with that performance. If that doesn't pull her toward you like a magnet, I don't know what will."

I turned my head to gaze in the black girl's direction and noticed she was walking back toward our end once again.

"See?" Hannah said. "You've obviously tweaked her interest. Let's see if she says hello."

As the girl moved closer toward us, I could feel my pussy throbbing, but when she reached the end of the pool, she glimpsed at me briefly then continued on to the end of the platform, disappearing into the sauna room.

"*Well?*" Hannah said, peering at me with raised eyebrows. "What are you waiting for? That's an invitation if I ever saw one."

"Yeah?" I said, still not convinced. "Are you sure?"

"She was watching you the entire walk back toward our end of the pool. Then she goes into a private room in full view of you. I don't think you need a crystal ball to know that she wants you."

"Okay," I said. "Should I bring a towel or something to cover up?"

"Was *she* wearing a towel?" Hannah said sarcastically.

"Fine. But if I'm not out in twenty minutes, come check up on me to make sure I haven't passed out or something. I'm feeling so light-headed right now, I'm afraid all that hot steam might make me collapse at the knees."

"I'm quite sure you won't need any help from me," she said. "But if she happens to come out first and I don't see any sign of you within a few minutes, I'll make sure you haven't fainted from all the pleasure you're about to receive."

"Wish me luck," I said, slowly rising from my chair, trying not to make it too obvious to everybody else in the room that I was following the girl into the sauna.

When I got to the room, I swung open the door and saw her sitting on the upper bunk with her left knee propped up on the bench, exposing her pink slit. Another woman rested on the bench directly beneath her, leaning back against the wood planks with her hands resting by her sides. I took a position kitty-corner to them on the lower bench, then leaned back against the wall with my opposite leg propped up, concealing my pussy.

I lay my head back and closed my eyes, pretending to relax and enjoy the hot steam. But when I opened them briefly and peered in the black girl's direction, I saw her right hand positioned in front of her pussy, moving her fingers in slow circles below her mound.

Holy shit, I thought. *She's playing with herself in full view of me!*

At first, I was so shocked at her brazen act of exhibitionism that I looked away, thinking she wanted to watch me only when she knew I wasn't looking. But when I peered back at her a few moments later, her legs were spread even further apart, exposing her beautiful pink vulva against her chocolate-brown skin. As her hand began to move in faster circles over her clit, her mouth parted open and I could hear her panting softly.

I glanced down at the other woman sitting below her who still had her eyes closed, oblivious to the ministrations of the sexy girl sitting directly above her. Feeling the sticky juices building up between my legs, I lowered my right hand into my lap and began rubbing my clit behind my propped-up leg. I didn't feel comfortable exposing myself fully in case the other woman opened her eyes, but I gazed directly back at the black girl as we massaged our clits.

As I began to feel the sweat dripping over my forehead and the pleasure spreading throughout my body, I slowly lowered my raised leg and spread my thighs apart, showing the girl my dripping pussy. She grabbed one of her tits with her free hand and pinched her long nipple while she stared at my glistening snatch. Before long, both of us were moaning softly, jilling ourselves with increasing fervor.

When I glanced down at the other woman to make sure it was still safe, I was surprised to see that she also had her legs spread apart and was rubbing her pussy as she watched me playing with myself. But at this point, I was too far gone to stop what I was doing, and knowing that the we were all aligned with our intentions, I began to moan and twist my hips on the warm cedar bench. When the black girl thrust her hand inside her pink folds and began thumping her back against the wall in rising pleasure, I couldn't resist the temptation any longer.

I rose from my bench and walked directly in front of her, positioning my head between her legs, then I pulled her hips hard into my face, eating her pussy like it was my last meal. She placed her hands behind my head and pulled me toward her, squeezing my head between her powerful thighs. As I reached up to grab her tits, I felt the woman's hand from below probing my slit, then she placed two fingers thrust inside me. While I moaned into the black girl's cunt, I lifted one foot and placed it on the bench beside the other woman and I felt her lips suck my erect clit into her mouth.

With my face buried in the black girl's snatch and my own pussy being serviced from below, I moaned into her cleft, feeling my orgasm approaching like a freight train. When it slammed into me, I groaned loudly into the girl's pussy, and she grabbed my hair while she clamped her thighs tightly against the sides of my head, quivering on the edge of the bench.

She held me in this clenched position for so long I was afraid she might suffocate me, but I dared not come up for air while she was in the throes of a powerful orgasm. After many long seconds, she finally loosened her grip and relaxed her legs then she leaned forward, thrusting her tongue into my dripping mouth. As we kissed each other passionately, the woman below removed her fingers from my pussy and I heard the sound of her breathing beginning to escalate while she attended to her own needs.

For the entire time the three of us were in the sauna, none of us had said a single word to one another. I didn't even know the *name* of the girl whose cunt I'd just finished eating out. There was something about this anonymous, no-strings-attached, down-and-dirty spa that I was digging. It didn't look like Hannah would have to save me after all.

For the first time since entering the spa, I felt completely liberated, ready to explore all the carnal opportunities on my own.

4

———

Feeling a bit awkward after my fling in the sauna, I left the room soon after and headed back over to my spot by the pool. I saw Hannah taking a leisurely swim, so I headed over to the juice bar and picked up two smoothies. When I returned to my lounge chair, I glanced around the room, soaking up the scene. With so many sexy women prancing around the place, I was surprised more of them weren't hooking up.

Maybe they're just self-conscious about making out in public, I thought. *Or maybe they're waiting for someone to break the ice.*

I glanced over in the direction of the hot tub, noticing a small group of women chatting and laughing in the bubbly froth.

If that's not the perfect place for a little extra-curricular activity, I don't know what is.

Hannah emerged from the pool and walked toward me, wringing out her hair.

"*So?*" she smiled. "How did it go in there? Did you finally get your freak on with your African goddess?"

"It definitely got pretty hot," I nodded.

"Like, almost *pass-out* hot? I'm a little disappointed you didn't call for reinforcements. Try as I might to attract the attention of other women in this place, everybody seems to be ignoring me."

I glanced at Hannah's naked body, admiring her tight, shapely figure. There was no reason she shouldn't be connecting with other girls, and I felt a little guilty for abandoning her.

"Maybe you just need a little extra *lubricant*," I said. "The hot tub in the corner looks like it might be more conducive for some close-quarter mingling. Do you want to give it a go?"

"Sure," Hannah said. "But don't you need a little time to recover? What happened to your girlfriend?"

"It seems she was only interested in one thing," I shrugged. "But I *could* use a little rest."

I pointed to the tall glass resting on the table beside Hannah's chair.

"I brought you a smoothie. Why don't we cool off before jumping back into the fire?"

Hannah patted her hair dry with a towel then lay back in her chair, taking a sip of her smoothie.

"So, have you had your eye on anyone *else* in this place?"

"Not really," I said. "Just about everybody looks seriously fuckable. I wouldn't mind wrapping my legs around that cute blonde masseuse though, if I had a chance. But I'm guessing that's against the rules."

"I dunno. What's good for the goose is good for the gander, in a manner of speaking. Maybe you just need to get her alone someplace."

"Perhaps I can schedule a *one-on-one* massage next time," I said. "I'm pretty sure I could persuade her to participate in a more interactive session if I had her all to myself."

"So you're thinking of coming *back*, then?" Hannah smiled. "Have they got you hooked already?"

"It's pretty hard to ignore a place like this," I nodded. "I wonder if they have monthly memberships?"

"The amenities would seem to fit that model. It's almost like more of a *health club*, with a few extra perks. Albeit some pretty fucking *awesome* perks."

"Speaking of," I said, peering over in the direction of the girls in the hot tub. "Are you ready to check out some of those other amenities?"

"Absolutely," she smiled. "If I can't hook up with someone there, at least I should be able to get some *other* kind of stimulation in the Jacuzzi."

We picked up our unfinished smoothies and carried them over toward the hot tub. When we got there, I noticed there were already four women submerged in the bubbling water and I wondered if there'd be enough room for Hannah and me.

"Have you got room for two more?" I asked.

"Absolutely," one of the girls said. "The more the merrier."

The women pressed their bodies closer together, and Hannah and I scooched in next to them. The water was warmer than I expected, but it didn't take long for me to get used to it, especially with the fleshy bodies of the other women rubbing up next to me.

"I haven't seen you guys here before," a forty-something redhead said, smiling at me. "First time visiting our spa?"

"Yes," I said.

"What do you think so far?"

"It's definitely a different kind of experience," I nodded, not yet ready to reveal just how *much* I'd actually enjoyed it.

"Have you availed yourself of any of the special services yet?" she said.

"Hannah and I had a couples massage a little while ago. It was very invigorating."

"Yes, those masseuses really know how to pinpoint the right spots," she smiled. "I'm Amber by the way."

I scanned her pretty face, admiring her piercing green eyes and high cheekbones. Although she was slightly older than most of the other women in the spa, she was equally as stunning, reminding me of the pretty runway model, Angie Everhart.

"Jade," I said. "And this is—"

"Hannah," Amber nodded. "Nice to see some fresh meat in this place, what do you think girls?" She peered around her, nodding at the other women in the tub, roughly her same age. "This is Kat, Anna, and Tammy."

"So are you guys–" I said, wondering if they came here often.

"Old fogies?" Amber laughed. "Yeah, I guess you could say we're regulars. There's more than *one* way to stay young at heart, you know."

"Speaking of," her friend Kat smiled. "We noticed you and that pretty black girl checking each other out earlier. Were you finally able to consummate your little courtship in the sauna?"

"Um..."

"It's okay," Amber chuckled. "We know *everything* that goes on in this place. Why else would we have lifetime memberships?"

I huffed softly, not quite sure how to respond.

"So are you two–?" Amber said, glancing at Hannah.

"No," Hannah said, shaking her head. "We're just good friends."

"That's a shame, because you look like a perfect match. Two pretty girls, one a blonde, the other a brunette. What are you, like barely *thirty*?"

"That's very generous," Hannah chuckled. "Just a little north of that. Maybe this invigorating spa treatment is beginning to work it's wonders already."

"There's a good chance. But you look like you could use a little extra stimulation. While your girlfriend's been improving her circulation in the steam room, you've been left to your own devices. There's a special spot over here where you can have some extra fun if you want."

"Oh?" Hannah said, suddenly perking up.

"I've been sitting right in front of it this whole time. Would you like to give it a try?"

"Sure," Hannah said, happy to have attracted the attention of some other women finally.

"Come," Amber said, standing up in the pool. "Let's switch positions. You come sit over here next to Kat and I'll sit next to your pretty girlfriend."

While Hannah and Amber switched positions, I took a moment to check out Amber's body. She had plump breasts with surprising firmness for her age and well-toned arms with tight, supple skin. Her wet hair draped over her lightly speckled chest and with her flushed cheeks and erect nipples, I found myself unconsciously spreading my legs trying to increase the flow of swirling water over my throbbing pussy.

When Hannah sat in her vacated spot, Kat suddenly reached under the water, pulling her legs forward a few inches, and Hannah's face lit up.

"*Right?*" Amber smiled, pressing her body up next to me. "I told you you'd like it. There's nothing like an invigorating water jet massage directed to the perfect location. Are you feeling more comfortable now?"

"Oh *yes*," Hannah grunted, shifting her hips closer to the pulsating underwater stream. "This is way better than the usual sex toys I'm accustomed to."

"And the best part is there's no *cleanup* required afterward. You can get off and freshen up at the same time."

"Mmm," Hannah moaned, surrendering to the feeling of the powerful spray stimulating her clit.

Suddenly Kat turned her body toward her and reached under the water, caressing her tits.

"Uhnn," Hannah groaned, turning her face toward Kat as they began kissing.

"Now *that's* a beautiful sight, don't you agree, Jade?"

"Absolutely," I hummed. "This is just what Hannah needed."

Amber placed her hand under the water and extended her arm toward my crotch. When she felt my fingers moving softly over my clit, she lowered her hand a few inches lower, thrusting two fingers into my hole. I didn't know what it was about this place, but I didn't seem to mind the members taking these kinds of liberties with my body. Between the swirling water jets pounding against my hips and Amber's sexy body rubbing up against my breasts, I was more than ready to ramp things up.

"That's a nice tight cunny you have," Amber purred. "Shall I continue?"

"Yes please," I moaned, flitting my eyelids in pleasure.

Amber suddenly raised herself off the bench and turned around to face me, straddling my hips and pressing her mound into my stomach.

"Mmm," she purred, pressing her melons against my tits. "You're *soft*, too. Do you like watching your girlfriend getting off under the water?"

"Yes," I panted.

With the four of us now actively engaged with each other, Tammy raised herself off her seat and sat down over Anna's thighs, facing the rest of us. Apparently, nobody except Amber wanted to miss catching the rest of the action in the hot tub while we groped and caressed one another.

Amber reached behind her back with her hand, cupping my trembling hand as I massaged my pussy. Then she placed three fingers inside me, fucking me while I stimulated my clit. She leaned in to kiss me, and I felt her hips tilt as she began rocking her pussy against the top of my mound. The idea of being fucked by this sexy older redhead while she rubbed her big tits against my breasts excited me tremendously, and before long we were tongue-fucking each other as we moaned into each other's mouths.

I peered over at Anna and Tammy, whose eyes were glazed over watching the rest of us as they rubbed their vulvas together with Anna squeezing her friend's tits from behind. Then I glanced over at Hannah and saw that Kat had angled her body toward her with one leg resting over her thigh, trying to get in on the powerful stream now pulsing toward both of their pussies. She smiled at me, nodding at how pleased she was with the turn of events.

With the heat in the hot tub beginning to ramp up, Amber and I began pressing our hips together more vigorously as our moans began rising in pitch in volume, and I could feel myself veering on the precipice, ready to pop off any second. Sensing I was close, Amber pressed her palm harder against my fluttering hand while she stroked my G-spot with her three fingers. Then she pressed her little finger further down my perineum until it rested against my pucker. While she moved her hand in circles overtop of mine, I spread my legs further apart, moaning loudly into her mouth.

"Yes," I grunted, feeling myself falling over the edge. "You're going to make me cum, Amber. *Oh my God–*"

As my orgasm washed over me, Amber pressed her little finger into my rosebud, and my entire perineum began clamping down over her hand.

"Yes, baby," she purred. "Let it go. Come for Momma."

I could feel her press her pussy more forcefully into my stomach as she rocked her hips with greater urgency, gripping my hips with her thighs.

"Uhnnn!" I cried, consumed with pleasure as I watched the other girls reaching their apex at the same time.

When the six of us finally stopping grunting and groaning, I looked around the spa and noticed that virtually everybody else in the poolroom had suddenly paired up, enjoying their own little moment of bliss.

5

———————

fter the wild ride in the hot tub, I needed some alone time, so I headed to the exercise studio to stretch and relax. Finding it empty, I walked over to a large padded mat against the far wall and sat down, pulling my hands toward my feet to loosen my leg muscles. The entire room was lined in floor-to-ceiling mirrors, with equal parts dedicated to aerobic classes, weight machines, and stretching. I remembered seeing aerobic classes on the list of services at the front desk, and I smiled at the thought of everybody's boobs bouncing up and down as they went through their paces.

No wonder everyone in this place is so fit and toned, I thought. There weren't many places in the spa where you could avoid being seen or seeing your own naked body from just about any angle. *There's virtually nowhere to hide or cover up.*

As I moved through my usual yoga poses on the mat, I watched myself in the mirror. I was proud of the tight figure I'd been able to maintain over the years, and I smiled seeing the muscles flexing in my arms and legs while I strained to hold the poses. But stretching in the buff was a whole *different* experience, and I felt my nipples hardening and my pussy moistening as I watched my tits and glistening vulva in the glass.

While I held my toes high off the mat balancing on my ass in a split-leg position, suddenly the door swung open and a familiar face entered the room. It was the pretty blonde from the massage room. She glanced at my exposed pussy reflecting in the mirror and smiled when I lowered my feet, closing my legs to protect my modesty.

"Don't stop on my account," she said, taking a position on the mat a few feet to my side. "A woman with your physique shouldn't be afraid to reveal every part of her glorious figure."

"Thanks," I said, leaning forward to rest my breasts on top of my thighs. "I didn't want to be too bold. I already feel exposed enough in this place as it is."

"You shouldn't feel self-conscious in here," she said. "That's the beauty of this spa. It's a place where women can go to free their minds and spirits without feeling judged in any way."

"It seems that's not the *only* thing that gets freed in this place," I smiled, alluding to our intimate session earlier in the day. "I had no idea I'd be releasing my inhibitions in so many different ways."

"*Jade*, isn't it?" she said, pinching her eyebrows together. "I remember you from this morning's massage."

"Yes," I said, blushing softly.

"I'm Julie," she said, reaching out to extend her hand. "We were never properly introduced."

"No, I suppose not," I said, feeling the hairs on my arms standing on end as I touched her for the first time. "I guess we were too preoccupied with other things."

"Mmm," she nodded. "Have you enjoyed your visit to our spa so far?"

"Oh yes," I said. "It's far surpassed my expectations. It's been a feast for the senses in so many ways. So much so that I needed to come in here and wind down for a few moments."

"I know what you mean," Julie said. "I like to come in here to stretch and meditate between appointments. I find it very therapeutic."

I watched her in the mirror as she twisted and contorted her body into increasingly difficult poses.

"How long have you been working here?"

"Only a couple of months. It's nice that the management allows us to use the facilities along with the rest of the members and guests."

As she moved through her stretches and poses, I marveled at her tight, lithesome figure. She was more slender than me, with smaller but firmer breasts and long, sinewy muscles that flexed sensuously as she went through her motions. When she leaned forward and lifted herself off the mat into a crow position, I admired her flexing arm muscles supporting her weight. But when she shifted into an inverted arm balance with her legs curved up over her shoulders, I couldn't help peering between her legs at her exposed slit.

"I always found that pose one of the tougher ones to hold," I said, feeling my pussy growing wetter by the moment.

"The key is to place your arms far enough apart with your legs positioned forward," she said. "Then slowly tilt your weight until you feel yourself balanced on your hands. Why don't you try it with me?"

She dropped her legs to the floor, then placed her hands and feet on the mat in a bent-over pose.

"You start in this position then gradually shift more of your weight over your hands. When you feel like you're supporting most of your weight on your arms, curl your legs forward and raise your feet off the floor."

I followed Julie's lead, panting heavily as I strained my arm muscles trying to support my weight.

"That's it," she nodded, seeing me raise my ass off the floor. "Now cross your ankles in front of your arms to lock yourself into position."

When I finally achieved the position, it felt surprisingly easy to hold the pose with everything held neatly together.

"That's excellent," Julie smiled. "It's not so difficult when you get into the right position, is it?"

"No," I puffed, staring at her pretty tits pressing together in the bent-over pose.

"Do you want to try something a little more challenging?" she asked.

"Okay," I said, feeling the cool air from below flowing over my exposed pussy.

"Keep your weight balanced over your arms, then unlock your ankles and extend your legs straight out in front of you until they're parallel with the floor."

I followed Julie's direction, grunting loudly as I felt the pressure building on my arms.

"Remember to keep your weight shifted forward so you don't fall back."

After a few seconds of struggling, I managed to achieve the pose, albeit with slightly crooked legs.

"That's fantastic, Jade," Julie said, peering at me in the mirror. "Why don't we take it one step further and see if we can shift into the firefly position."

Julie angled her legs higher in the air, tilting her ass toward the floor until her legs were pointed forty-five degrees up in the air, with her entire body balancing on her outstretched arms. With her pussy staring directly in front of me between her splayed legs, it took all of my concentration to stay focused on executing the technique.

"I'll try," I panted, feeling some drops of lubrication falling onto the mat between my legs.

With my legs pointing forward as much as I could, I slowly lowered my hips toward the floor, balancing my suspended weight over my arms until I matched the angle of Julie's upturned legs. I could feel the strain in my hamstrings from my legs pulled back behind my shoulders, and I glanced in the mirror, seeing the reflection of the bright overhead lights reflecting off my glistening, wet pussy.

"You got it, girl!" Julie said, peering between my legs. "How does it feel?"

"Strangely invigorating," I grunted, running my eyes all over Julie's body in front of me. "But this is killing my hamstrings. I think I need to loosen up a bit more before trying some of these more advanced poses."

"Absolutely," she nodded. "You don't want to hurt yourself. Let's give your muscles a rest before you pull something."

I lowered myself onto the mat then placed my hands beside my quivering legs, breathing heavily in and out.

"That was exhilarating," I said, peering over at Julie. "You've obviously got many talents beyond massage therapy."

"It's all part of the mind-body connection," she smiled. "Strength, flexibility, relaxation. It keeps us healthy in many different ways."

I glanced at her perfect tits glistening with sweat, feeling my pussy throbbing in excitement.

"If this is what it takes to achieve your level of fitness, I'm all in. I don't think I've seen another woman with as perfectly toned a figure as yours."

"You're no slouch yourself, Jade. It's just a matter of building up your stamina. Do you want to try some *partnered* stretching to loosen up your muscles a bit more?"

I'd been waiting for a chance to pair up with the pretty masseuse, and when she indicated she was ready to move to a new phase in our routine, I suddenly became aware of the puddle forming on the mat between my legs.

"As long as you promise not to twist me into a pretzel this time."

"No worries," she smiled. "This next one is super simple and far more relaxing. All you have to do is sit on the mat with your legs extended in front of you, with your feet spread apart a few inches. I'll face towards you with our feet touching together, then we can hold hands and gently pull each other forward and back to stretch the back of our leg muscles."

I nodded, imagining myself rocking back and forth with her in whole *different* kind of position.

Julie shifted her body around in front of me, and when she spread her legs and touched her feet to mine, I felt a surge of electricity coursing through me. I had to fight hard to keep my gaze above her neckline as she smiled and reached out her hands toward me.

"Now bend forward one inch at a time while I hold your arms. When you feel the tension in the back of your thighs, breathe deeply and try to relax until you feel the pressure receding."

I was able to bend forward far enough to clasp her hands, and I smiled when she squeezed me gently.

"Now, let me pull you slowly toward me until you feel tightness in your hamstrings again. Stop me when it begins to bind, then breathe slowly in and out until you feel your leg muscles relax."

I did as she instructed, and after a few minutes Julie was able to pull my upper body almost parallel with my legs resting on the floor.

"There you go," she nodded. "Now let's see if we can do the same thing with the adductor muscles on the inside of your thighs. I want you to spread your feet slowly apart as I maintain tension on your arms. You should feel pressure in the muscles on the side of your crotch as you begin to lengthen the tendons on the inside of your legs."

"I definitely feel *something* there," I huffed, watching the slit between Julie's legs open wider and wider the further I pressed my legs apart. She glanced between my thighs, noticing the wet spot on the mat directly in front of me.

"Remember to go slow," she said. "You definitely don't want to pull *this* muscle. This one's pretty important for maintaining sexual health and flexibility."

"You don't have to remind me twice about that one," I smiled. "I definitely don't want to put a damper on that."

"Okay, now lean back and begin to pull *me* forward now. This way we can *both* benefit from this stretch while we pump the blood through our muscles in this area."

"Yes," I purred, pulling her upper body toward me as we pressed our feet further apart. "I feel my circulation improving already."

The more we pulled our bodies toward one another, the further our legs pressed apart, bringing our pussies closer together and our bodies closer to touching. But just as her face moved to within inches of my throbbing snatch, the gym door swung open and two women paused at the entrance, seeing us in the compromising position.

"Do you mind if we join you?" one of the girls said, staring at the glistening reflection of my wet pussy.

"I'm good if you are, Jade," Julie said while I felt her breath inches away from my dripping pussy.

"Of course," I said, not wanting to throw a wet blanket on our fun. "There's lots of room on the mat for more people."

The girls sat down beside us, assuming a similar position.

"That stretch looks interesting," the first one said. "It certainly looks more stimulating than doing it alone."

"It's even more fun to perform it as a *group*," Julie said. "Why don't we form a circle with our feet touching and see if we can stretch and loosen our muscles *together*?"

She shifted her ass back a few inches then spread her legs further apart, inviting the girls into the circle. They positioned themselves next to us, then Julie spread her arm to her side, clasping the hand of the girl next to her. I did the same until we were all holding hands with our legs forty-five degrees apart, touching our feet in a chain-link circle.

"Well now that we're getting to know each other a little better," the first girl said. "I suppose we should introduce ourselves. I'm Taylor and this is Quinn."

"Pleased to meet you," Julie said. "I'm Julie."

"Jade," I said, nodding to each of the girls.

"So how does this work exactly?" Taylor said, glancing down at the juices coating the inside of my thighs.

"Jade and I were pulling each other to stretch our hamstrings and adductor muscles. But in a perfect circle, we'll be maintaining equal pressure between the four of us, so in order to move closer together, let's try spreading our legs further apart."

As we all followed Julie's instructions, our circle slowly began collapsing into a diamond shape.

"That's the idea," Julie said. "Can you girls feel the tension between your legs the closer we get to one another?"

"Yes, and that's not the *only* thing I'm feeling," Quinn said, glancing at our glistening pussies coming closer together.

"When we get close enough to our partners," Julie said, "reach out and clasp her hands, pulling you closer together. As you rock back and forth, you should be able to spread your feet further apart, slowly releasing the tension on the inside of your thighs."

"Mmm," Taylor groaned. "I feel it. How close should we try to get to one another?"

"As close as possible," Julie smiled. "If you can relax your adductors enough, ideally you should be able to touch in the middle."

As the four of us pulled each other closer and closer, spreading our legs further apart, Julie's upper body began to bend over my hips with her tits edging tantalizingly close to my throbbing pussy. I glanced at Taylor and Quinn, whose feet were pressed against the sides of Julie's and mine, and they smiled at each other as they peered between each of their open legs. Before long, both couple's glistening pussies were only inches apart as we pulled our upper bodies closer toward our hardening nipples and parted mouths. When I felt the strands of Julie's hair caress the top of my breasts, I pulled her harder toward me and she encircled one of my teats in her mouth.

"Mmm," I groaned, trying to spread my legs into a one-hundred-and-eighty-degree split, desperate to feel her pussy up against me.

But after a few moments, she began pulling me in the opposite direction. As I leaned forward over her tight abdomen, I licked my tongue up the crease in the center of her stomach until I reached the base of her tits. Then I sucked her medallions into my mouth, circling her nipples with my tongue, and she tilted her hips forward, touching our vulvas. I moaned loudly into her breasts when I felt our juices intermingling, but as soon as our clits touched, she suddenly leaned forward, pressing her body back in my direction.

I was beginning to go crazy with all this reciprocal teasing, wanting to feel Julie's lips against my own as we ground our pussies together. By now, all four of us had our legs spread into a virtual split, with the original circle collapsed into two parallel lines. Growing impatient, I pulled Julie hard toward me until her body rested on top of me, and she began kissing me as we rubbed our tits and vulvas together. This time, there was no desire for either of one of us to separate while we ground our wet pussies together, rubbing our hard clits over one another.

"Fuck yes," I purred into her mouth. "This is insanely hot. Rub your body against me, Julie."

"You've reached the height of your flexibility," she nodded. "Now just try to relax your muscles while you let the rest of your body enjoy the experience."

"Oh yes," I panted. "I'm definitely shifting my concentration to *other* parts of my body."

I peered at Taylor and Quinn out of the corner of my eye and saw that they were similarly commingled, rubbing their pussies and tits against one another with their legs spread wide apart.

"Uhhn," I heard them groan next to Julie and me.

There was something incredibly sexy about the four of us touching our feet together while we rubbed our bodies next to one another, listening to the mounting passion generated between the four of us. I tilted my head up a few inches and looked in the mirror in front of us. With Julie's legs splayed wide apart and our mounds joined together, I saw both of our slits spread open as our juices rolled down over each other's vulvas. I'd never seen anything so sexy in all my life, and the fact that we were engaged in a two-way affair with Taylor and Quinn right next to us just added to my excitement.

I began to feel the pleasure rising inside me and with our hands no longer needed to pull ourselves together, I wrapped my arms around Julie's back and thrust my tongue into her mouth, feeling my climax edging closer. When it finally hit me, I groaned loudly in Julie's mouth, spraying my juices over her vulva and ass while she grunted simultaneously inside my mouth. As the four of us writhed and groaned on the mat in simultaneous union, I heard some movement by the door and glanced up to see a large group of women pausing at the entrance, with their mouths wide agape.

It didn't take long for them to rush toward us joining us on the mat, rolling together in a giant heap of naked, writing bodies. As we intertwined our arms and legs, sucking and rocking against whatever body part presented itself to each of us, I smiled realizing I'd reached a new kind of nirvana. Something told me this spa was about to become my new go-to gym for the foreseeable future.

VOLUME THREE

THE TOY PARTY

1

———————

"How goes the practice?" I asked my best friend and certified sex therapist, Hannah, over lunch. "Any interesting new cases?"

We were meeting for our weekly catch-up at our favorite restaurant on Chicago's Navy Pier overlooking Lake Michigan. With our busy schedules, it wasn't always easy for us to find time to nurture our longstanding friendship. But I could always count on Hannah to share some juicy tidbits from her private practice during our two-hour break every Wednesday.

"Never a dull moment," she said. "You'd be surprised at the endless variety of dysfunctions people come to me with. Just yesterday, I had a young woman worried about her excessive squirting when she orgasms."

"Is that a problem?" I said. "I mean, isn't that a *good* thing? I squirt sometimes when I come too, but it's usually after a long buildup and during an unusually powerful orgasm. Most of my partners find it to be a huge turn-on."

"That's what I tried to tell her. I explained that it's perfectly natural for many women and that she shouldn't worry about it. She thought she was literally peeing on her partners during sex."

I choked on a salad crouton in mid-swallow and quickly washed it down with a gulp of water.

"Just to be clear, though—it's *not*, right? There's a lot of misconceptions about vaginal squirting. I don't want to feel self-conscious about it—"

"No," Hannah chuckled. "You needn't worry about spraying your lover with an unintended golden shower. Ninety percent of the time, it's just the ejection of your natural lubrication when your vagina contracts during orgasm. As you suggested, whenever it happens it's usually a sign of exceptional internal wetness and/or unusually strong contractions."

"And the other ten percent of the time?"

"Some women expel a secretion from the Skene's glands, located next to the urethra. And yes, in very rare circumstances, one can become temporarily incontinent and expel a small amount of urine. But it's all healthy organic fluid, and in all cases an indicator of a powerful orgasm. Most women should be thrilled to experience that kind of 'dysfunction'. The more common problem is the lack of ability to orgasm at all."

"Really?" I said, watching some dark clouds roll in from the east side of the bay. "I thought that was mostly limited to heterosexual couples where the man doesn't know how to properly stimulate his partner."

"That's common, yes. Most guys can't find a woman's clit with a magnifying glass. But honestly, most of the time it's because the woman has some kind of mental block. Either she grew up learning sex was something to be ashamed of or she had an early traumatic experience. The latest studies show that seventy-five percent of women can't orgasm from intercourse alone and up to fifteen percent can't come at all."

"How do you help them overcome their problem, if you don't mind my little play on words."

"Actually, that boils it down to the core of the problem. They have to learn how to break down the barriers stopping them from achieving climax. First, I teach them that pleasure is a natural part of the sexual experience, designed to encourage procreation. Then I tell them the best way to experience orgasm is to stop trying to orgasm. It's like a guy who can't get it up when the chips are down—they're feeling too much pressure to perform. I encourage them to find a quiet place where they can explore their bodies without any distractions then lose themselves in the journey of discovery without worrying about the destination."

"Alone?"

"At first, yes. There are too many expectations when you bring a partner into the equation. They have to learn how to break down the walls restricting their freedom of expression before they can let others into their intimate space."

I nodded, reflecting back on my own first time experiencing sexual pleasure. It was when I was taking a bath and I discovered how good it felt to let the water from the faucet flow over my pussy. From that day forward, I experimented with endless types of self-stimulation. By the time I had my first fling with a high school boyfriend, all my hang-ups about sex had been thoroughly dispelled.

"What about when they return to their sexual partners? Is there even such a thing as a vaginal orgasm? What happens to the *other* seventy-five percent who can't come with their husbands?"

"That whole vaginal vs. clitoral orgasm concept that Freud first introduced is a total myth," Hannah said. "It wasn't until about twenty years ago that scientists properly mapped the full anatomy of the clitoris. Did you know that over ninety percent of the clitoral structure is actually *inside* the vagina? The tiny glans and shaft on the outside are just the parts that we can see. There's no reason why a woman can't experience a penetrative orgasm if properly aroused and stimulated by a caring partner."

The sun suddenly broke through a hole in the clouds, casting a spotlight over the nearby grounds in Millennium Park. The chrome skin of the famous bean-shaped sculpture glistened in the light, reminding me of my favorite U-shaped vibrator.

"Is that what happens when we stimulate the G-spot?"

"Partly. The G-spot corresponds to the location of the underside of the shaft of the clitoris. It's a bit like the sensitive frenulum on the underside of a man's penis. But the rest of the clitoral structure surrounds much of the vagina, which is why it feels good even when we're having missionary sex. We're all born with the same genital anatomy. It's not until around the third month of prenatal development that the structures deviate into the familiar male and female forms."

My panties began to dampen as I began to think about all the new ways I could explore my pussy with my large collection of vibrating dildos.

"Fascinating," I said, shifting restlessly in my seat. "Do you ever encourage your clients to experiment with *sex toys* to mix things up if they're still having trouble making it work?"

"After a while, yes. But first they have to get in the right frame of mind. It's not an exaggeration to say that the brain is the largest sex organ. A lot of women can actually *think* themselves to orgasm. You've got to be *mentally* aroused before you can achieve physical excitement. I don't want my clients to become too dependent on the artificial stimulation of a sex toy before learning to enjoy sex the natural way. No partner can hope to match the intensely focused stimulation of a sex toy. At its core, sex is designed to be a social activity to ensure procreation."

I slammed my knife and fork on my plate and stared at Hannah in mock indignation.

"Don't tell me you're one of those sexist shrinks who still believes sex is only meant to be enjoyed between a man and a woman under holy matrimony."

"Of course not. We humans have thankfully evolved to the point where we can enjoy sex for its own sake. You know me better than that. I consider myself to be pansexual. I enjoy and encourage all forms of sexual expression. Gay, straight, bi, transgender—whatever turns your crank. Life's too short to be worried about all that hypocrisy about only one proper way to experience sex. So if using toys helps you spice up your sex life and keeps your relationships fresh and exciting, I'm all for it."

"Cheers to that," I said, raising my glass of sangria.

"To *hump day*," Hannah winked, clinking her glass against mine.

"You know, all this discussion has got me thinking. I feel like I've grown so much since my boring marriage ended a few years ago. My sex life is so much more enjoyable now that I'm open to having sex with other women. And my house is a veritable sex toy museum. I've often thought about inviting some of my closest friends over for a toy party. You know—to share the *wealth*, as it were. Would you be willing to give a little talk about some of your insights on sexual health? I'm sure there's a lot of other women who could benefit from your knowledge and experience."

Hannah peered across the table at me with a raised eyebrow.

"Were you intending for this to be a 'hands on' party, or just an educational meeting?"

I paused as a small curl formed at the edge of my lips.

"I was thinking we could start out as an informational forum and see where it goes from there. You could share your knowledge of sexual anatomy and mental health while I demonstrate the latest advances in sex toy development. If some of the ladies want to practice some of their learnings and avail themselves of the available sex aids, I don't see why we should want to stop them. Are you down for that?"

Hannah took another sip of her wine as she peered over the rim of her glass with fluttering eyes.

"Sounds like it could be fun. Knowing you, I have a feeling this little party will soon devolve into a full-blown orgy. But I've never experienced one of those, so count me in."

"Good," I said. "I'll send out the invites later today. Are you available next Saturday?"

Hannah reached into her purse and pulled out her phone. I could tell even before she checked her schedule from the way she was squirming in her chair that she was already committed. She tapped the screen twice then looked up at me and smiled.

"I think I can make that work."

I could barely contain my excitement on the drive home thinking about how I would organize our get-together for maximum enjoyment. Part of me was genuinely looking forward to educating my friends about all the cool sex toys I'd discovered in my journey of sexual exploration since my divorce. But I definitely had another agenda. There were a few girls I'd had my eye on for some time who'd rebuffed my subtle advances. Whether it was because they professed to be 'happily married' or because they just weren't into lesbian sex, I had a feeling this party would tear down whatever remaining walls they might have to expanding their sex lives.

I knew full well that some of the toys I'd be demonstrating would tempt more than one fence-sitter into wanting to try them out right then and there. I just had to create the right atmosphere. By the time I pulled into my driveway, my car seat was soaked in a puddle of wetness under my burning crotch. I raced upstairs and flipped open my laptop, starting a new email message with the subject *Girl's Slumber Party*. With trembling hands, I began composing my message:

Dear friends,

This Saturday, I'll be hosting a most unusual and exciting party. The theme of the gathering is 'sexual health and wellness'. I've invited my good friend and registered sex therapist, Hannah Bristol, to give an informative presentation on the latest developments in the area of women's sexual health.

A big part of this is learning to relax and explore our bodies in a safe and nurturing environment. To this end, I've invited another friend, Cheryl Clifton from the local branch of the Babeland adult emporium chain to demonstrate some of the exciting new sex toys they've recently introduced. You're encouraged to learn, experiment, and dabble to the extent you feel comfortable.

This is a girls-only party. Leave your husbands, boyfriends, and other cockadoodles at home. Dress comfortably—it'll be our own little slumber party. Come one, come all!

RSVP by Friday p.m.

See you all soon,

Jade xo

As I began to fill in the To: field with the email addresses of my friends and associates, I paused after entering the names of the obvious candidates. It went without saying that I would invite the women I'd already shared a private tryst with and those who I knew to be lesbians. But half the fun would be trying to entice my stanch heterosexual friends to drop their britches along with everyone else.

By the time I finished filling in the list of addressees, I'd assembled an eclectic list of twenty friends and acquaintances, all of whom I'd be happy to fuck at the slightest provocation. I paused for only a millisecond before tapping the Send button. Then I tore off my pants and plunged my favorite rabbit vibrator dildo deep into my pussy. As I slid down in my chair spreading my legs wide apart, I closed my eyes imagining what it would be like to watch twenty sexy women pleasuring themselves while the rest of us looked on.

2

———

By Saturday afternoon, I was already dripping in anticipation of the coming festivities. Almost everyone I'd invited had RSVP'd that they were planning to attend. The only person I still hadn't heard from was the hot housewife who lived on the opposite side of my back yard. I'd caught Alana stealing lingering glances at me from her upper deck whenever I lay around my pool in my bikini. But her needy husband always seemed to be hanging about, and we'd never managed to find any private time together. Tonight, I had a special plan for how I might entice her over to my place.

I'd arranged the guest chairs in a semicircle in the middle of my family room, with two additional chairs in front of the arc, facing the backyard window. One of the chairs would be reserved for the official presenter—first Hannah, then Cheryl. I would sit in the second chair providing color commentary. But most of the 'commentary' I was planning to provide would be more *visual* than verbal. I knew the only way I was likely to get the rest of the women to sample the vibrators would be if I demonstrated how some of them worked myself.

There wouldn't be enough replicas of each vibrator for every participant to try them at the same time, but between the many different types we were planning to show, there'd be more than enough to keep everyone entertained. And unlike most other sex toy shops' policy of offering no returns of purchased products for hygienic reasons, each woman at *our* party would be welcome to share and pass along their toys for the pleasure of the other participants.

Beside each chair, I'd placed a container of alcohol wipes and a fresh towelette so everyone could safely clean each device before reuse. I didn't want anything stopping the ladies from being willing to experiment and enjoying themselves to the fullest. The last thing I did to set the mood was draw the drapes and turn the dimmer switch down. I wanted just enough light to create a playful atmosphere while still providing enough visibility for everyone to watch one another.

In front of my own chair, I left the curtains parted a small crack with a direct line of sight to Alana's balcony. There wouldn't be enough space for someone outside my fenced yard to make out what was going inside with an unaided eye. But using the spyglass I'd often caught Alana using behind her kitchen window, she'd be able to zoom in on the action all she wanted. After dusk, the light from inside my house would create the effect of an illuminated stage in a darkened theater. Everybody else's privacy would be safely protected facing away from the window. But Alana would have a bird's-eye view of me displaying all of my favorite toys.

As my friends began to arrive, we shared some wine and cheese and made small talk about the latest developments in our work and personal lives. Nobody wanted to broach the subject of our planned activities for later in the evening, but by the time the last attendee arrived, everybody was nicely loosened up by the free-flowing alcohol. I invited everyone to take a seat in the semicircle, while Hannah and I took adjacent chairs facing the group. Hannah had brought a small case with her that she placed it on the floor beside her chair.

"Good evening everyone and welcome to our little get-together," I said. "It's great to see all my close friends together once again. We seem to find it more and more difficult these days to make time to commune with our busy schedules. We've got an interesting theme for tonight's gathering, and I've invited two close friends to make a presentation in the context of women's sexual health. I think you'll find the planned festivities will be both mentally and physically stimulating."

As I began to make eye contact with the women around the room, they smiled nervously back at me. I was sure many of them had no idea what they were getting themselves into.

"Some of you already know Hannah, a registered sex therapist who has been counseling women in her private practice for almost ten years. I think you'll find she has some interesting insights and experiences to share with us. I've also invited my good friend Cheryl Clifton, who is the owner of the Chicago Babeland adult store on Michigan Avenue, to show us some of the fascinating new sex toys that have recently come to market."

I glanced toward Cheryl and she raised her arm to acknowledge her presence. Some of the ladies nodded toward her, recognizing her from their previous trips into her store.

"Hannah," I said, who was sitting beside me. "Did you want to start things off with a few opening comments?"

"Thanks, Jade," Hannah smiled. "Jade and I were talking the other day over lunch about some of the concerns many women still have about their sexual health. She thought it might be fun to share some of our mutual experiences and learnings in a safe and learning environment."

She reached down and opened the case beside her and pulled out an unusually shaped stuffed toy.

"I didn't want to get overly formal about what should be a fun subject, so I thought I'd try to lighten the mood using my favorite puppet."

She placed her right hand in the back of the stuffed toy then held it up for the whole room to see. Many of the women giggled when they recognized the familiar shape and features of a woman's vulva.

"Hi, I'm Valerie, the vagina puppet," Hannah squeaked in a playful voice. "While I may not be proportioned to the correct relative scale, I think you might recognize some of the familiar features on my body."

Hannah caressed the velvety sides of the puppet framing the organ like two puffy parentheses.

"These are the labia majora," she said. "Their job is to cover and protect the more sensitive internal parts of the vagina. Though I must say I rather enjoy having this part of me stroked and caressed as a prelude to deeper exploration of my body."

Many of the women around the circle chuckled as they watched Hannah playing with her puppet. But they shifted uncomfortably in their seats as her fingers moved closer toward the inside of the faux vulva.

"These thinner folds are the labia minora. They're even more sensitive to touch than my larger siblings and can get quite wet when properly stimulated. Their purpose is mostly to provide a slippery surface for easy penetration of a man's penis, but I like to insert *other* phallic-shaped devices inside me when the mood strikes. These lips also connect at their top edge to the clitoris and help provide some very pleasant friction during vaginal thrusting."

Hannah placed the fingers of her left hand over a puffy red ball at the apex of the inner folds. Then she flipped up a flap of silk covering the nub and smiled.

"And this is the hood of the clitoris that helps protect this super-sensitive organ when it is not in use."

She pinched the fingers of her left hand together and inserted them into the opening of the vulva, thrusting her hand gently in and out. The silky hood of the clitoris pulled back and forth over the nub as she stroked her pretend pussy.

"Notice how the hood pulls forward and back over the glans as the labia minora are stretched and contracted with each penetration."

Some of the ladies around the arc crossed their legs and squeezed their thighs excitedly together, becoming aroused by the vivid depiction of their private anatomy.

"Many women think they can't come just from penetrative sex," Hannah continued. "But this design is intended to increase the stimulation on our most sensitive organ even from indirect touching. Did you know that the clitoris is the only organ in either a man's or a woman's body with the sole purpose of providing pleasure? And that the head of the clitoris has over *seven thousand* nerve endings—even more than in the glans of a man's penis? So much for penis envy. If guys had any idea how good it feels to stimulate a woman's clit, they'd gladly switch places with us."

Everyone in the group laughed out loud and nodded in agreement, starting to loosen up.

"But here's the really interesting part," Hannah said as she angled her puppet from side to side for all the women to see. Surrounding the vulva behind each of the labia majora were two puffy 'wings' connected to the outside shaft of the clitoris, making it look like an inverted wishbone.

"The clitoris is actually far larger than many of us believe. The little nub and shaft on the outside is just the tip of the iceberg."

She lifted the two wings framing the internal walls of the vagina to reveal a larger pair of puffy tissues.

"These tissues extend inside and around the walls of the vagina and connect directly to the clitoral shaft and glans. The thinner flaps are called the *crura*, and the puffier tissues underneath them are the *bulbs*, corresponding in many ways to the corpora cavernosa in the shaft of a man's penis. They're all part of the greater clitoral structure, extending more than four inches around each side of the vaginal wall at rest."

Many of the ladies leaned in closer as their eyes widened in surprise, realizing for the first time just how large and all-encompassing this sensitive part of their anatomy was.

"The male and female genitalia both develop from the same embryonic structures," Hannah continued. "They don't actually differentiate until fairly late in fetal development. Just like a man's penis, these structures swell and extend fifty to three hundred percent when stimulated. So the next time someone tells you there's no such thing as a vaginal orgasm, don't believe it. A woman should be able to come just as easily from proper internal stimulation as from external manipulation of the outside glans."

Recognizing that some of the women were eager for the next

phase of the demonstration, I signaled to Hannah that it was time for a shift in the discussion.

"Thank you, Hannah, for that entertaining and enlightening explanation of a woman's sexual anatomy. I don't know about you guys, but I'm feeling a lot more empowered about my sexual health knowing that my lady cock is just as big and powerful as any man's."

The women around the circle cheered and clapped their hands excitedly, equally surprised and impressed with Hannah's presentation.

"What do you say we put Valerie away for a little while and focus on learning some the interesting ways we can stimulate our *real* peachkas now that we understand a little better where all the interesting parts are?" I nodded toward Cheryl and she switched places with Hannah, placing a much larger case on the floor in front of her. "Cheryl is now going to demonstrate the almost infinite varieties of toys we can use to stimulate our wonderful flower in the privacy of our own homes."

"Or with a partner," Cheryl suggested. "I think you'll find these sex aids are equally stimulating used either alone or as part of communal play. There's no reason why you shouldn't be able to introduce some of these toys into your partnered sex life to keep it vibrant and interesting."

I smiled at her and winked, happy that she'd planted the seed for broader group exploration.

She reached down and flipped open her case. Inside, was a treasure trove of multicolored and unusually shaped toys. She picked up two phallic-looking objects of different sizes.

"Following on Hannah's illumination of the shape and structure of the clitoris," she said. "Women's sex toys fall into two general categories: internal and external."

She held up the smaller object and turned it around in her hand for everyone to see.

"This little guy may look familiar to many of you as the trusty 'pocket rocket' vibrator. It's only about two inches long and less than an inch in diameter, but it packs quite a wallop for its small size."

Cheryl ran her fingers teasingly over the nubby end of the finger-sized device.

"You can place these ridges overtop of your clit and twist the tube to select one of three different vibration settings."

She twisted the shaft of the pocket rocket and the device began to hum with a soft whine.

"The good news is that you can carry this guy around in your smallest purse and use it fairly discreetly, since it's no bigger than your index finger."

She pulled two more pocket rockets out of her case and handed them to the women at opposite ends of the semicircle.

"Feel free to pass these around and see what they feel like as you experiment with the different settings. This is what I like to call our 'entry-level' vibrator. It's very basic, but it definitely does the job."

I pulled my own pocket rocket out of the pocket of my jeans and placed it playfully between my crotch.

"If any of you want to see what it actually feels like against your clit," I said, "don't be shy about giving it a try. Clothes on or off, this is a judgement-free zone. We're all liberated ladies here and I don't want anybody to feel self-conscious about enjoying each of these toys to their fullest limits. You'll notice that I've placed some alcohol wipes and clean towels beside every chair, so you can safely and comfortably clean each device after each use."

"And that's another point I want to make about sex toys in general," Cheryl chimed in. "Different toys are made out of different materials. But some are more *hygienic* than others. You should always buy toys made out of medical-grade silicone or hard plastic. Avoid any device made out of a soft jelly or rubber. These materials have thousands of microscopic pores that trap bacteria and can spread disease. The other types are easily cleaned with regular soap and water, or alcohol wipes if you want to be really safe. It goes without saying that all of the toys we'll be demonstrating here tonight use the safe, non-porous materials, so feel free to experiment away!"

As the women passed the little vibrators around the circle, some of them held it in their hands experiencing the different vibrations, while others pressed it gently between their legs as their eyes widened in surprise.

"Pretty powerful for such a little device, isn't it?" Cheryl said, nodding toward the more adventurous ladies. "But this is really just the most basic of sex toys. There's been a surge of innovative new designs to hit the market over the last couple of years."

She reached down into her case and picked up a donut-sized device with two pointy ends that looked like rabbit ears.

"This is the *Form 2* clitoral vibrator made by JimmyJane. The lovely thing about this sex toy is that you can place these two little fingers on opposite sides of the shaft of your clit to receive a heavenly stimulation, almost as if someone is stroking you with their hand. It's got a quiet but powerful internal motor that you can quickly recharge using the available charging cable. Unlike the pocket rocket, which uses a regular double-A battery. So you'll need to keep plenty of replacement batteries on hand to be sure you don't run out of power at the worst possible time."

Cheryl handed two models of the Form 2 vibe to me and I passed them to the girls in the middle of the circle.

"This one is best appreciated with a minimum of layers between you and the device," I hinted.

I nonchalantly unzipped my jeans and pulled them down to the floor, then slipped my own Form 2 vibe under my panties. A few of the girls raised an eyebrow at my bold gesture, but it didn't take long for them to refocus their gaze at my midsection as they watched me squirm and grunt from the pleasant sensations emanating between my legs.

Most of the other women were also wearing jeans and were reluctant to drop their leggings as they pressed the vibe gently against the seam of their pants. But a few had come prepared with skirts and summer dresses, and I watched excitedly as they slipped the two-pronged device under their hems and began to moan in pleasure. Unfortunately, nobody seemed quite ready to carry their self-stimulation to the ultimate peak and come in full view of the others as they politely passed the two devices around the circle.

Recognizing their hesitation, Cheryl reached into her toy case and pulled out another vibrator. This one looked like a small egg with two grooves on top and a little O-shaped loop connected to the end. She slipped her index and middle fingers through the loop and cradled the egg in the palm of her hand with her two fingers resting inside the grooves.

"This interesting device is called the *Fin*, manufactured by Dame Products, a female-founded and female-run adult toy company. The nice thing about this vibrator is that you can use it almost like an extension of your own hand. It's great to use in couples play to bring an extra level of stimulation to your partner. It's also equipped with a rechargeable battery and provides a quite satisfying sensation to the outer clitoris and overall vulva area. I happen to have four of these on hand, so I'm going to pass these around for more of you to enjoy."

Cheryl handed another one to me and smiled.

"As usual," she said, "Jade will be demonstrating some of the many ways you can use this for maximum enjoyment."

I placed the Form 2 vibrator over my hand then pressed my fingers under the top lip of my panties. As I felt the buzz spread over the head of my clit, I closed my eyes and spread my legs, sinking down in my chair. As I began to feel the rising tide of pleasure spread over my pelvic region, I opened my eyelids a slit and noticed three other women had unzipped the front of their jeans and had the palm of their hands gently rolling over their vulvas. As the rest of the girls squirmed in their seats looking on, the four of us mewed in obvious delight from the sublime tingling between our legs.

Feeling a bit sorry for the other girls being left out of the fun, I pulled the vibe out of my panties and tapped the button to turn it off.

"I'm saving myself for the *next* one," I winked. "I have a feeling Cheryl is getting ready to pull out the heavy guns."

Cheryl smiled at me as she reached into her case and pulled out a much larger device with a plum-sized ball attached to the end of a long handle.

"Right you are, Jade," she said. "This one has the generic name of magic wand and is made by various manufacturers, but my favorite version is this one with the trade name *Le Wand*. This is a major league vibrator, with a deep, penetrating rumble and twenty different vibration settings. It's not to be taken lightly, as it can set you off in a matter of seconds and can be quite addictive. You might want to be careful about pulling it out when your husband or boyfriend is around, since they might be more than a little threatened by both its size and how powerful it is."

Cheryl clutched the head of the device with her hand and twisted the round ball on the top.

"It's got a flexible neck, which makes it feel a bit more natural and it also comes with a bunch of fun attachments."

She reached into her bag and pulled out a variety of odd-shaped covers, placing each one over the end of the wand.

"This nubbly cover," she said, running her fingers over the spiny surface, "feels a bit like a French tickler when pressed against your vulva.

"Whereas *this* attachment," she said, replacing it with a cap having four large protruding nubs, "is billed as a deep tissue massager. But of course, it has much more interesting *sexual* exploration uses."

Then she reached into her case and pulled out a cone with a large curved finger extension.

"But this is my favorite attachment. It's perfectly shaped to stimulate the G-spot on the inside front surface of your vagina, and it will take you to an entirely different level. I'm going to hold off on passing this attachment around because we're going to have a special demonstration of the internal vibrators soon."

Cheryl turned to me with a devious smile.

"Jade, would you like to have first dibs at demonstrating this little gem?"

She passed me one of the wands and handed two others to the women at the edge of the circle.

"I thought you'd never ask," I said with a wicked grin. "But this time I don't want anything getting between me and my vibrating friend. If you girls don't mind, I'm going to get buck-naked to properly enjoy this thing."

As many of the women around the circle widened their eyes in shock, I pulled my panties all the way down to my ankles. Then I flicked the switch on the side the wand and placed it against the front of my vulva, holding it with two hands.

"Fuck, yes!" I purred as the vibrator began to rumble between my legs.

I noticed it was starting to get dark outside and glanced through the crack in my curtains, recognizing some movement on the balcony across from my back yard. Just as I'd suspected, my neighbor Alana couldn't resist spying on me to get a closer look at what was going on inside. I couldn't tell if she was holding her binoculars, but I spread my legs as wide as I could as I rubbed the bat-shaped vibrator between my legs. If she was watching, I planned to give her a show she'd not soon forget.

Suddenly, I heard some moaning coming from the other ends of the circle and I turned my head to see the other women had thrust their magic wands down under their panties and were gripping the handle tightly as they rolled their hips sensuously in their chairs. I locked eyes on one of the girls, a married friend who'd previously been reluctant to share details about her sex life with her husband. As Heather and I began to feel the swell of pleasure sweeping over our bodies, we grunted and groaned in delirious pleasure.

Most of the other women who were without a vibrator had already shoved their hands down their pants or under their skirts as they watched the three of us tremble in our chairs. When Heather gaped her mouth wide open and began to shake uncontrollably in her chair, I couldn't hold back any longer. My orgasm overtook me and I grunted loudly as I hunched over, convulsing in ecstasy. Suddenly, the room was filled with the soft sighs and moans of twenty oversexed women losing themselves in the pleasure of intense self-stimulation as we watched each other rise to the culmination of pleasure.

3

———————

Seconds after I came, the doorbell rang. I was tempted to ignore it, but the interruption provided a welcome distraction from the awkwardness of twenty women peering at one another with their hands still down their pants. I threw on a robe and scampered up to the front door and looked through the peephole. It was my neighbor Alana, fidgeting self-consciously on the doorstep. I smiled for a moment, then swung open the door.

"Sorry I'm late," Alana stammered, staring at my curvy body wrapped up in the robe. "I had to finish making dinner and cleaning up after my husband. Have I missed much?"

I looked down at the wet patch in the crotch of her jeans and knew that she'd been touching herself as she watched me through the drapes.

"Not much," I said. "Come on in. We're just getting started."

I led Alana back to my family room and pulled up an extra chair at the edge of the circle.

"This is my neighbor Alana," I said, not wanting to interrupt our flow with a long introduction. "She was held up with a few unavoidable distractions, but better late than never to our party."

I motioned toward Cheryl, who was cleaning the wand I'd just used with an alcohol swab.

"This is my friend Cheryl from the Babeland store in downtown Chicago. She's been demonstrating some of the latest offerings from her establishment. Make yourself comfortable. We were just starting to get to the interesting items."

I looked at Cheryl and smiled.

"What other exciting toys have you got in that magic box of yours?"

"I'm glad you asked, Jade," Cheryl said. "I was just getting ready to demonstrate our line of *internal* vibrators."

She reached down into her case and lifted up two familiar-looking dildos. One had the traditional shape of a pointy pink cucumber and the other looked like an oversize erect penis.

"Until recently, these were the only kinds of internal vibrators that women had to choose from. One's shaped a bit like a pickle and is made out of hard plastic. The other one looks like a super-veiny cock, and is made out of soft silicone. While both come equipped with a handy internal vibrator, their designs are not very inspiring and, just like a man's cock, have limited functionality."

The lesbians around the circle chuckled, but more than a few of my straight friends also nodded, acknowledging their dissatisfaction with their one-dimensional sex lives. I glanced at Alana and she smiled at me nervously as a light blush spread over her cheeks.

Cheryl placed the vibrators back in her case then lifted up another dildo shaped like a banana with a little bump on the end.

"This is called the *Gigi* vibrator, from Lelo," she said. She turned the device slowly in her hand, stroking the tip teasingly. "It has a gentle curve and a specially shaped tip that makes it perfect for stimulating the G-spot."

Cheryl looked toward Hannah and smiled.

"Hannah, would you like to demonstrate how to properly position this device using your little puppet?"

Hannah lifted her stuffed toy off the floor then slowly inserted the curved vibrator into the puppet's hole with the little bump facing up.

Then she pressed the shaft downward, angling the tip toward the inside front surface of the vagina.

"As you can see," Cheryl said, "this vibrator is much better suited to stimulating the sensitive G-spot than a straight dildo. And the best part is that it's whisper-quiet, so you can use it discreetly in the privacy of your own bedroom without your husbands being any the wiser. Some women find it's easier to insert with a bit of lube, so we've placed a tube of body-safe cream beside everyone's chair if you want to give it a try."

As before, Cheryl passed one of the vibrators to me and three other girls in the circle. The women turned the wand curiously in their hands as they experimented with the different vibration settings, not quite ready to plunge it into their pussy in full view of the other participants.

Recognizing their apprehension, I flipped open my robe and spread my legs apart. I glanced over at Alana and noticed she had her legs crossed as she squeezed her thighs together while staring at me with wide eyes.

"I don't know about the *rest* of you," I grinned. "But I'm still pretty wet from using the last vibrator. Screw the lube—I'm ready to get *fucked*."

I inserted the dildo deep into my pussy and angled it upward, then turned the vibration setting up all the way.

"Holy shit!" I growled. "This feels absolutely heavenly. You girls have *got* to give this a try. Remember, what happens in Jade's house, stays in Jade's house. We're all big girls and this can stay between us. No one else needs to know how much fun we really had at our little sorority party. Feel free to take off your pants and dresses and get your groove on!"

Two of the women holding the Gigi vibrator looked at one another for a moment, then they pulled their jeans down simultaneously, inserting the wand between their lips. They pressed the shaft in about four inches and angled it downwards as their eyes rolled under their lids and they slithered down in their chairs. I looked at the third woman, who'd slipped the vibrator under her dress, concealing it under her panties. But within seconds, all three of them began moaning and panting as they grasped the handle of the wand and thrust it firmly inside their pussies. I glanced at Alana, who had her hand down the front of her pants as the stain on her jeans spread further down her thighs.

The sight of so many women playing with themselves as they watched our glistening dildos plunging in and out of our pussies raised my excitement to an entirely new level, and I moaned loudly as I began to feel my passion rising. Within minutes, the four of us were trembling in our chairs as we watched each other fuck ourselves with this magnificent tool. As I began to feel the familiar tingling feeling spreading throughout my pelvic region, I spread my legs further apart and began to groan uncontrollably.

"Fuck—that feels so good," I said, shifting my gaze between the three women. "I'm going to cum soon. Are you girls getting close?"

They all nodded as their moans began to rise with a heightened urgency and their eyes glazed over. When one of the girls suddenly slumped over in her chair and pulled her legs together, shaking convulsively, I groaned as I felt the contractions inside my pussy clamping against the shaft of the vibrator.

"I'm cumming!" I hissed, pulling the vibrator hard up inside me, pressing it firmly against the front of my cunny.

"Yes—Yes!" one of the other girls panted as she also began to quake in her chair.

But I was most turned on by the sight of the girl in the summer dress shaking in her chair as her mouth silently spread open and a deep rash washed over the top of her chest. By now, Alana was rubbing her clit furiously under the front of her jeans, and it didn't take long for her to slump forward, trying unsuccessfully to conceal the look of ecstasy on her face. Even Cheryl and Hannah were getting in on the action as they plunged their fingers deep inside their pussies.

After we all came down from our highs, Cheryl composed herself and sat back up in her chair.

"I knew you guys would enjoy that one," she said, trying to collect her breath. She panned around the room and made a mental note of who still hadn't had a chance to use one of the sex toys. "I see there's still a few of you who've been left out of the fun. Let's see if this next one might entice you into the fold, in a manner of speaking."

She reached down into her bag and lifted up another large penis-shaped dildo. But this time, two projections looking like little fingers protruded from the device about halfway up the shaft.

"Some of you ladies might recognize this little baby made famous by Samantha on Sex in the City. It's called the *Rabbit* because of these cute little ears that stick out from the side of the vibrator. But this device can stimulate you in so many other ways."

She flipped on the switch at the base of the unit and little chrome-colored beads began circulating around the middle of the translucent shaft. "These rotating balls provide quite a lovely sensation when you have it inserted inside you." She flicked another switch and the tip of the vibrator began rolling like a bobble head. "This vibrator might not be curved like the *Gigi*, but if you angle it properly inside your vagina, the twisting head does almost as good a job stimulating your G-spot."

Many of the women around the circle nodded, having had first-hand experience with the toy.

"But the best thing about this vibrator are these little rabbit ears," Cheryl said, flicking the two flexible flaps on the side of the device. "If you place them directly over your nub, you can get a full-body orgasm from the simultaneous stimulation of your inner and external clitoris. There's a reason why this is a staple in just about every woman's bedroom—it's the definitive multipurpose dildo for today's liberated woman. I've got two more of these to share with the girls who haven't yet had a turn, and I know Jade also keeps one of her own in her private collection."

I smiled at Cheryl as I pulled my brightly colored rabbit vibrator out of my bag resting on the floor.

"Damn straight, girl," I said. "This is my number one vibrator whenever I go on vacation, and I also keep it handy in the night table right beside my bed. This little guy has given me many an intense orgasm over the years. It's quite a special little toy. Although in this case—" I smirked, stroking the shaft, "it's not so *little*."

The girls laughed as I switched on my Rabbit and it began to whirl and roll like some kind of possessed robot-cock. Cheryl handed the other two vibrators to the women near the middle of the group, and I was disappointed not to see one of them passed to Alana. But I knew we still had a couple more toys to show, and I was confident that by the end of the evening she'd be fully participating like the rest of the girls. I was glad to see another one of my straight girlfriends holding one of the rabbit vibrators in her hand, and she looked at me devilishly as she smiled with a wide grin.

"You might want to use a bit of lube with this one," I said, looking at my gyrating vibrator in mock trepidation. "It's considerably bigger and girthier than the others, and you might find it slides in a little easier with a bit of help."

I picked up my tube of lube on the floor and squirted a healthy dollop up and down the shaft of the device, placing a few extra drops on the wide head. Then I placed the dildo between my legs and ran it up and down the inside of my labia to entice the other women to take off their clothes. Within seconds, the other two women had taken off their jeans and panties and were mimicking the movement of the dildo between their legs. As I watched their chests beginning to rise and fall in pleasure, I inserted my Rabbit into my hole and slowly pressed it further inside until the rabbit ears rested against my clit. When I felt the fingers trilling against my button, I sloped down in my chair, grasping the end of the dildo with two hands.

"This is one hell of a magic cock, don't you think ladies?" I grinned. "Who needs a man when you've got one of these to play with."

By now the other two women had inserted their Rabbits deep into their pussies and were nodding vigorously in agreement. The sight of two big vibrating dildos planted deep inside their snatches was an incredible turn-on, and by now almost all the other women had removed their clothing and were jilling themselves unabashedly as they watched the three of us fucking ourselves with our big vibrating cocks. I glanced over at Alana and saw that her jeans were now resting around the base of her ankles with her fingers rotating under the front of her panties. I smiled at her and nodded, moaning approvingly at her loosening inhibitions.

I was still buzzing from my last orgasm, and it didn't take long for the feeling of impending climax to spread over my body as I watched the rest of the girls grunting in their chairs. But this time I didn't want to come so fast that I couldn't enjoy everybody else's experience to the fullest. I bit my lip and pulled the vibrator slightly away from my clit, concentrating on the feeling of the rotating beads and gyrating head moving inside me.

I wasn't sure if the other two girls had used a Rabbit before, but from the expression on their faces, they looked like they were having a transcendental experience. As their passion began to rise, I watched their bodies progressively tense up as they gripped the shaft of their big dildos with two hands and pulled it harder against their vulvas. I could see the rabbit ears flapping against their clits as they thrust the vibrating cock harder and harder inside their pussies until they both began to whine at the onset of a powerful orgasm.

"That's right," I encouraged, "let it go, girls. Let me watch you cum all over your big dildos. I'm going to cum with you."

Suddenly, the three of us wailed out loud as a powerful orgasm washed over us while we held the big dildos tightly against our vulvas, our legs stretched out in front of us, convulsing in a long simultaneous orgasm. I heard a squeal coming from the other end of the circle and I turned my head just in time to see Alana thrusting her fingers deep inside her cunny as she mimicked our action, lost in her own powerful orgasm. I smiled at her as we both shook deliriously in our chairs.

4

It was hard to imagine getting any higher than this from any other of Cheryl's toys, but she smiled at me with a devious grin as she pulled her dripping fingers out of her panties. I was a little disappointed that she hadn't yet removed all of her clothes like most of the other ladies, but I guessed she wanted to maintain some degree of modesty while she continued her demonstration. After pausing a while for everyone to recover from their last episode, she reached down into her case and lifted up a U-shaped device with two flattened ends.

"I know you're all probably thinking it can't possibly get any more intense than that," she said. "But I've been saving the best for last. This interesting little device was developed by a woman who wanted to feel something different from the typical vibrator. It's called the *Osé*, by Lora DiCarlo. Unlike just about every other sex toy, this one doesn't have a conventional vibrating motor. Instead, it *undulates*, mimicking the feeling of a human touch on your vulva."

She turned on the device and it began to writhe in her hand like an animated snake.

"This end of the device flexes in a *come-hither* motion as if your partner is drawing his or her fingers gently against the inside of your G-spot.

Every woman, including myself, leaned in and squinted their eyes, mesmerized by the unusual movement of the toy.

"At the same time," Cheryl continued, "this end of the device slithers with a *pulsing* motion that mimics the feeling of a tongue licking the glans and shaft of your outer clit."

"Holy shit!" I said, shocked at the innovative design of the toy.

Cheryl turned her head toward me and nodded.

"Even *Jade* hasn't tried this one yet. It's just literally come onto the market and we're one of the few stores to be given exclusive distribution rights. Since none of you have tried it yet, I'm going to take the liberty of showing you how it works *myself* before I hand out a few extra models."

Cheryl lifted her hips off her chair and slipped her panties down to the floor, then raised her feet to shed the lower half of her clothes.

"As you can see," she said, holding the device directly in front of her separated legs. "This toy is shaped in the form of a 'U' and can be used hands-free once properly inserted. The fatter end goes inside and the thinner part rests on top of your outer clit."

She angled the device so the bottom of the U was facing the circle of women, then she inserted one end into her hole. As she gently pressed it upward, the thinner end slid up her vulva until it rested firmly over her clitoral shaft.

"There are two buttons on the bottom edge of the Osé that you can use to easily adjust the pace of the undulations."

She placed two fingers on the bottom of the U and tapped each one in turn.

"The button with the *Plus* symbol on the right-hand side increases the speed and the button with the *Minus* symbol beside it lowers the speed. But you won't notice a buzzing or throbbing sensation like the other vibrators. The buttons simply change the pace and rhythm of the undulations, much like your partner does when he or she adjusts the way they're licking and stroking you."

I could hear a gentle hum emanating from between Cheryl's legs as she spread her thighs apart and closed her eyes, concentrating on the feelings inside her.

"Before I get too lost in the pleasure provided by this incredible toy," she said, briefly opening her eyes, "I'm going to pass out three more models to the group. Please hand them along to those who haven't yet had a chance to test one of our vibrators. If I'm doing my math right, this last toy should cover the remaining girls who haven't yet had a try. But don't worry, ladies—you'll be glad you saved yourself until the end. This is one amazing sex toy that you won't soon forget."

Cheryl handed me three Osé toys, and I passed one to Alana and one to my straight friend Barb, keeping the last one for myself.

"You know what might be kind of fun this time," I smiled, noticing a few of the girls still partially covered up. "Is if we remove *all* of our clothing so we can watch and enjoy each other fully unencumbered with any camouflage. I don't know about the rest of you guys, but I get just as turned on *watching* your bodies as I do by touching myself. If you're all feeling comfortable enough, let's shed the rest of our trappings and revel in the beauty of our feminine bodies!"

It didn't take long for every single woman around the room to take off the last vestiges of their clothing. Even Alana had dispensed with the last of her inhibitions as she pulled off her blouse and unclasped her bra behind her back. I panned around the semicircle, admiring the different shapes and sizes of all the sexy women.

"Let's get started then, shall we?" I said, winking at my friends.

Some of the girls still had a few of the earlier models of the sex toys resting beside their chairs and they picked them up as the three of us began to insert the curved Osé into our pussies. Those who didn't have access to a toy spread their legs wide apart and began to massage their clits with their fingers.

It felt strange slipping the unusual-shaped device inside my pussy, but as I pressed it further and further inside me, I hummed in satisfaction at the way it gripped my crotch. I almost felt like someone was cupping their hand over my vulva with their fingers touching my G-spot on the inside and their thumb resting over my

clit on the outside. But when I tapped the On button at the base of
the device, my eyes flew open in surprise.

Just as Cheryl had suggested, the sensation was unlike any other
vibrator I'd previously used. Instead of a concentrated vibration
sensation, the two ends of the device rolled and undulated against my
tissues in a most natural way. On the inside, the long end curved and
stroked me in a come-hither motion. On the outside, the other end
undulated over my bulb, teasing and caressing my clit with its
animated tongue-like action. I looked at the other two girls who had
the Osé embedded in their pussies, and they had an equally incredulous expression on their faces.

I smiled at Alana, and she responded by spreading her legs
further apart. I noticed the juices coating the inside of her thighs as
she rolled her hips sensuously on her chair and locked eyes with me.
The otherworldly feeling of someone touching me in my most sensitive areas was driving me insane, and for a brief moment, I fantasized
about our two bodies pressed together so we could enjoy the feeling
in unison. I knew this was likely the first time she'd had sex openly in
the presence of other women, and it didn't take long for her to begin
thrashing and moaning as she watched me and the other girls
enjoying themselves. After only a few minutes of stimulation from
her new sex toy, she suddenly threw her head back and screamed as
her thighs began flapping together from the intense contractions
washing over her. Not long after, Barb groaned equally loud as she
shook violently in her chair from the orgasm taking control of her.

Within seconds, virtually everyone around the room including
Cheryl and Hannah were squealing and shaking from the most erotic
show any of us had ever witnessed. I was the last one to shoot off, and
as I grabbed each of my tits in my hands, I gushed all the juices that
I'd been building up inside my pussy out the two sides of my ring all
over Cheryl and Barb, sitting directly in front of me. I sat convulsing
in my chair for almost a full sixty seconds as the rest of the women
watched in amazement. When I finally slumped forward in my chair,
completely spent and exhausted, everyone stood up and clapped
with a standing ovation.

5

____

After the three of us who'd used the Osé vibrator had come down from our highs, everybody looked at one another wondering what to do next. We were all dripping wet and buck naked, and nobody was in a hurry to end the party. But Cheryl had shared with me how she planned to step up each activity, and I knew she had one last trick up her sleeve that would bring everyone together in the end.

"That was fun, wasn't it?" she said, breaking the awkward silence. "It looked like some of you shared a pretty intense connection during that last demonstration. With that idea in mind, I had a few more toys to show you that were specially designed for multiple partner enjoyment."

She suddenly stood up and walked behind the sofa positioned against the far wall. She lifted an ottoman-sized object draped in a bedsheet off the floor and placed it in the center of the arc between the main group and our two chairs. Then she pulled off the cover with a flourish and threw it behind her. The device looked like a squat pommel horse, but in place of a saddle in the middle of the curved midsection were two diamond-shaped dildos pointing up about one foot apart.

"This strange contraption," Cheryl said, "is the *Sybian Sex Machine*, and it delivers quite a ride. It can be used by one or two people at a time, but as you can see from the double dildos positioned on top, it's best enjoyed as a partnered activity. Each person can face one another and caress the other as they receive powerful internal stimulation from the uniquely shaped dildos. The secure base of the unit allows both participants to ride the machine cow-girl style."

I panned around the circle and noticed the women looking at the device slack-jawed with wide eyes. It was obvious that few of them had seen or tried anything like it, but their erect nipples and swiveling hips suggested they were eager to give it a try.

"Those of you who like to have sex with a man once in a while," Cheryl smiled, "know that the girl-on-top position during intercourse allows for better control and provides a nice firm surface to rub your clits on. You'll notice this device comes with a vibrating pad under each dildo that delivers full-body stimulation to your entire vulva region. You really have to try it to appreciate it. Who'd like to volunteer to be our first test subjects?"

A few girls raised their arms and Cheryl pointed toward two women she recognized from their earlier trips into her store with their husbands. I was unsure if she purposely chose two straight girls to help break down their inhibitions about trying same-sex lovemaking, but I was nevertheless thrilled to see Dawn and Julie approach the device. They both had tight, athletic figures and I'd long fantasized about fucking one or both of them whenever we'd been out on group playdates together. I crossed my arms over my chest and pinched my nipples as I rubbed my legs together in anticipation of watching the two girls try the sexy machine.

"All you have to do is straddle the device," Cheryl instructed, leaning back in her chair holding a control box wired to the base of the unit. "Then sit down gently as you ease the dildos inside of you, facing one another. You might want to place a little lube on them first to make it go in a little easier."

She handed each woman a tube of lube and they generously lathered the dildos underneath them before sitting down over the plugs. The sight of the glistening phalluses disappearing into their neatly shaved snatches made the hairs on the side of my arms stand up on end. Suddenly I became aware of how wet my chair cushion had become as I watched the two women.

"How does that feel?" Cheryl said to the women.

They both made a soft mewing sound as they peered silently at Cheryl, afraid to look at one another and acknowledge that their naked bodies were mere inches apart.

"Can you feel the bulge in the middle of the plugs?" she asked. "They're designed to provide better stimulation of your G-spot once the action gets going."

"Um-hmm," Dawn nodded.

"Yup," Julie replied curtly.

"Let's see if we can make it a little more interesting," Cheryl said as she began to twist one of the dials on the control box.

A soft hum began to emanate from inside the machine, and the two women's eyes widened as they began to roll their hips unconsciously over the seat.

"Better?" Cheryl asked.

"Yes," Dawn panted, closing her eyes to concentrate on the buzzing feeling inside her.

"We've only *begun* to experience what this device can do," Cheryl winked.

She turned another knob on the control box, and the pads under the base of the dildos began to flap against the girls' clits. Julie gasped as she placed her hands behind her on the bench, unsure where to put her arms. Dawn crossed her arms nervously over her chest as she grunted and flitted her eyelids in pleasure.

"Feel free to touch one another," Cheryl said, trying to get the girls to loosen up and become more engaged with one another. "The whole point of this device is to revel in each other's pleasure and make it an interactive experience."

Dawn reached out tentatively and cupped each of Julie's trembling tits in her palms. Julie leaned forward and placed her arms around Dawn's back then the two women pressed their bodies together.

"There we go," Cheryl nodded. "Feel the pleasure coursing through each other's bodies as you caress one another. Lose yourself in the experience as you become one. We're going to begin ramping up the intensity level now."

She twisted both knobs further to the right then flicked a switch on the side. Each of the dildos suddenly began gyrating inside the women's pussies, pressing more firmly against the front of their tunnels. Both women groaned and locked lips, probing their tongues inside each other's mouths. As they began to mash their breasts together and moan in unison from the incredible sensation enveloping their pussies, I glanced around the room.

All the other women were playing with themselves in one form or another as they watched the sexy show in front of them. For my part, the sight of two straight girls rubbing their bodies together as they were being remotely stimulated by an innocent bystander was too much to resist. I picked up my rabbit vibrator off the floor and flicked the speed to max as I jammed it inside my pussy, pulling it hard against my tingling button.

"That's what I'm talking about," Cheryl purred, watching the two women beginning to lose themselves in each other's passion. "Are you ready to take it to the penultimate level?"

"Mmm-hmm," the two women nodded as they ran their hands over each other's bodies while they continued to kiss passionately.

Cheryl twisted the two dials to their maximum setting, and the hum inside the machine deepened as the flaps under their pussies began to flap wildly. Dawn and Julie pressed their hips forward, gyrating their hips together as they got closer and closer toward climax. Within seconds, they began wailing in tandem as their bodies shook violently with their arms clasped tightly around each other. Seeing the two women coming together soon put me over the edge also as my pussy clamped tightly over the vibrating shaft of my

Rabbit toy. I glanced over at Alana and noticed that she was holding a Form 2 vibrator over her clit while she quaked in her chair watching the other women in the room jilling themselves as they took in the action.

6

———————

After everyone had finished coming once again, Cheryl looked at the two girls still sitting on the now-silent Sybian machine.

"What do you think, ladies?" she said. "Does that feel anything like riding your husbands on top?"

"Fuck no!" Dawn said. "This is way better!"

Julie nodded enthusiastically in agreement, and everybody around the room laughed out loud.

"Well at least now you know how much fun it can be to play with some of your own kind," Cheryl said. "And while we're on that subject, I'd like to demonstrate a couple of toys that will allow you to be even *more* actively engaged with your same-sex partners." She peered at Dawn and Julie and smiled. "You guys are welcome to stay there if you wish or return to your seats for this next demonstration."

The two women kissed each other one last time then eased themselves off the bench, revealing two glistening, pearly-white dildos. When they returned to their seats, I noticed they were holding hands beside one another. I smiled at their new special friendship and nodded at them approvingly.

Cheryl moved the Sybian machine off to the side of the circle then reached back down into her display case. When she sat up, she revealed a giant flexible dildo with a raised ring running around the middle of the shaft.

"This is a two-sided or double dildo," she said, running her fingers over the two ends of the object shaped in the form of the head of a man's penis. "As you can see, it's a little longer than a regular man's cock and it has two heads for double the pleasure. Perhaps *most* interesting though, is this raised band in the middle."

She squeezed the shaft near the center and the band began flapping like the pads on the Sybian machine.

"When two women press this dildo inside them from opposite ends, the vibrating ring in the middle provides some very pleasant supplemental stimulation as they grind their pussies together. Unlike the Sybian machine, which you experience in more of a passive role, with this device you can actively fuck each other in a multitude of positions."

Cheryl looked around the room and smiled mischievously.

"Who'd like to give this one a try?"

Two of my lesbian friends raised their hands but I quickly preempted them. Watching Cheryl demonstrate her toys all this time had gotten me seriously worked up and I jumped at this opportunity to have some fun with her.

"I notice that *you* haven't yet had a chance to use any of your toys today, Cheryl," I said. "If you're game, I'd be happy to demonstrate this one for the rest of the group with your participation."

"I thought you'd never ask," Cheryl said, winking at me. "Let's get down on the floor and show these ladies how two lesbian women can get it on."

I lay down on the carpet in front of the chairs with my hips facing up and spread my knees apart. Cheryl lay down in a similar position facing me, with our vulvas about a foot apart. Then she squirted a drop of lube on each end of the dildo and pressed one end against her opening. As she shimmied her hips toward me, half of the dildo slowly disappeared inside her pussy. When the other end pressed against my hole, I mimicked her movement until the plug was fully inserted inside our bodies with our vulvas mashed together.

"Are you *in* yet?" Cheryl joked, lifting her head off the floor and peering toward me.

"Judging by the feel of your wet pussy pressing against mine, I'd say so," I meowed.

"Shall we get started then?" she said.

"By all means," I purred.

As we both began rolling our hips together, I felt the dildo thrusting in and out of me as it plunged deeper and deeper inside my cunt. Although it wasn't vibrating yet and it didn't have the beneficial shape of some of the other curved vibrators, the feeling of Cheryl actively fucking me with the unicock and the sensation of her wet lips grinding against mine more than made up for the lack of other features.

Suddenly, she rolled over onto her side and straddled me with one leg under my ass and the other one over my tummy. As she humped me more aggressively, she began to grunt like a wild animal. I was enjoying the experience of being on the bottom for a change, but just as I began to feel the familiar feeling of another orgasm rising up within me, she turned over another ninety degrees until she was facing face-down on the carpet.

"Fuck me from behind, Jade," she groaned. "I want to feel your ass slapping against mine."

"Fuck yes!" I said, quickly rolling over so we were both facing down.

We pulled our knees forward and lifted ourselves up until we were resting on all-fours with our butt cheeks pressing against one another. Cheryl reached between her legs and pinched the middle of the dildo, and the snake suddenly began writhing inside our pussies as the ring between our legs flapped against our two clits.

"Oh God," I moaned as Cheryl began rocking her hips against me, slapping her ass against mine.

The simultaneous feeling of the gyrating dildo in my pussy with

Cheryl's ass grinding against mine and the vibrating ring trembling against my burning clit felt incredible.

"*Fuck*, Cheryl," I hissed. "I'm gonna cum. I'm gonna cum so hard all over your pretty ass. Come with me baby."

"I'm close," Cheryl growled. "Spray all over my wet hole. Let me feel you cum all over my burning cunt."

Whether it was Cheryl's sexy dirty talk or the sensation of being watched by all the other women around the room, I felt my orgasm suddenly wash over me as I began to shake uncontrollably against Cheryl's ass. My pussy clamped down hard on the flexible dildo as I felt the juices squirting out of my hole all over her opening.

"Yes, Jade!" she wailed. "Spray me with your cum. I'm coming baby! Fill up my hole as you cum inside me!"

As we both pawed the carpet like two cats in heat, I heard the sighs of other women around me and turned my head to see every one of them fucking themselves with one device or another as they watched us, their breasts trembling as they came in simultaneous union with Cheryl and me.

7

———

A s the two of us lay spent and exhausted on the floor, I looked up at the other women peering at one another expectantly. It was obvious that they were ready to engage more actively with some of the others, and this seemed like the ideal time to open things up for broader participation. Cheryl and I looked at each other, thinking the same thing, and nodded.

"This seems like a good time for the rest of you to find a partner and try some interactive play," I said. "Feel free to grab whatever toy you can find and experiment away. It's always a lot more fun when you bring someone else into the mix, and there's a limitless degree of combinations you can create when you bring other partners into the equation. Grab a spot on the sofa, or use one of my private rooms, or join the rest of us on the floor. This party is a long way from being over!"

Almost immediately, all the other girls joined us on the floor, pairing up with new and old acquaintances, as they picked up various loose toys and rubbing them against each other's bodies. I peered over in Alana's direction and noticed that she was sitting by herself, looking at my naked body longingly. I turned to Cheryl, still joined at the hips with me on the floor, and she motioned for me to go to her. I pulled myself off my half of the dildo and Hannah quickly took my place, smiling at Cheryl as they pressed their hips together.

I was happy to see my friends hooking up and enjoying themselves so openly, but as I walked toward Alana crossing her legs shyly, I felt sorry for the one person in the group who still seemed hesitant to participate in the group fun.

"Haven't you been enjoying the party?" I said, taking a seat on the chair beside her.

"Yes, of course," Alana said, placing her arms shyly over her chest.

"I've noticed you participating at various times," I smiled. "But you seem reluctant to engage with the others. Are you feeling uncomfortable?"

"No—not really," she said. "It's just that no one else here...*interests* me."

I sensed what Alana was getting at, but I wanted to be sure before taking the next step.

"No one else meaning..."

"*You*, Jade," she said, peering into my eyes. "I've been watching you for so long, wanting to make love to you."

I slipped off my chair and kneeled in front of her, kissing her softly on her lips.

"I've been watching you from afar also, Alana," I said. "I've had many a sleepless night fantasizing about your beautiful figure, imagining myself touching and licking your naked body."

I lowered myself down the front of her body, nibbling the side of her neck and kissing the top of her chest. When I reached her firm breasts, I cupped each one in my hands and ran my tongue over her nipples in gentle circles. I could feel her nubs hardening in my mouth as I sucked on them gently. Alana tilted her head back and moaned, pressing her body toward me. As I moved in closer, she spread her legs further apart, and I could feel the heat emanating from her pussy.

Eager to feel her in my mouth, I continued lower until my face was level with her mound. I was a little surprised to find her so smooth and bare down there, and I looked up at her with a quizzical look.

"I shaved myself just for you," she said. "I didn't want anything coming between the two of us tonight."

I smiled up at her then rolled my cheeks against her soft pubis, flapping my eyelids with butterfly kisses against her skin as her thighs trembled in anticipation of my touch further below.

"Suck me, Jade," Alana whinnied, pressing her hips harder toward me. "I want to feel your lips on my most private parts. I've been dreaming about this for so long—"

Before she could finish her sentence, I lowered my face and encircled her flaming clit in my mouth, rolling my tongue over her pearl. Alana gasped and grabbed the back of my head, pulling me harder against her soaking vulva. I hummed in approval, alternating between flicking my tongue over her erect shaft and sucking her button deeply into my mouth. Her clit was larger than most, and I could feel her sex extend a full inch into my mouth as I sucked on her little cocklet.

Alana began rocking her hips wildly on her chair as she fucked my mouth shamelessly. Her groans grew progressively louder but just as I was sure she was about to come in my mouth, she suddenly pulled away and peered down at me with a possessed look on her face.

"I want to feel you inside me when I cum," she said. "Fuck me, Jade. Fuck me with one of Cheryl's sexy toys. I want to be your bitch."

I shook my head in shock, momentarily taken aback by Alana's newfound boldness. Whether this was simply her straight side wanting to get fucked in the manner she was accustomed to, or she was demonstrating her desire to adopt the femme persona in our new lesbian tryst, I didn't care. I just wanted to take her and consummate our long, lingering relationship as quickly as I could. My eyes darted along the floor to find something I could fuck her with, but seeing that all the other toys were in use by the other women engaged in heated affairs, I peered into Cheryl's case and noticed a strap-on dildo.

"Wait here, babe," I said. "I think I have just the thing."

I walked gingerly around all the writhing bodies on the floor and reached slowly into her case. Hannah and Cheryl were nearing the point of no return as they fucked each other wildly with the two-ended dildo, and they smiled at me devilishly as my breasts wobbled above their faces.

"Go fuck that girl," Hannah said. "Show her what it's like to experience a real orgasm."

I nodded at her then scampered back to Alana's chair where I found her already kneeling on the floor with her glistening ass pointed up toward me.

"Yes, Jade," she purred. "Fuck me with that big dildo. Let me feel your big cock deep inside me."

It didn't take more than a few seconds to wrap the belt around my waist and legs to secure the big phallus over my mound. It had a gentle downward curve and a thick head specifically intended for G-spot stimulation when used from behind. I noticed a couple of buttons on the front of the harness, but I was in too much of a hurry to feel Alana's pussy wrapped around my cock to figure out what they did. I reached between her legs to see if she needed any lubrication and she was slippery as a runny faucet. I pointed the tip of the dildo against her hole and wasted no time slamming it inside her cavern. If she wanted it rough, I thought, I was only too happy to oblige.

"Oh *fuck!*" Alana groaned. "That feels so good. Can you feel me squeezing you?"

I couldn't of course, because it was an artificial dildo. But I could feel the resistance of her tight pussy clamping against my faux cock as I pulled it out and slammed it back into her. The feeling of her ass cheeks slapping against my mound and my throbbing clit just amplified the feeling of fucking her like a man. I wondered what her husband would think if he knew what I was doing to his wife behind my closed curtains.

From her escalating moans and movements, I could tell that she was close to popping off, and I selfishly wanted to come with her. Maybe it was from me channeling the replacement of her husband or maybe it was just me desperately wanting to get off again. But either way, as sexy as it was to screw this little vixen with my artificial cock, I wasn't getting quite enough direct stimulation to get there with her.

I pulled out of her halfway for a moment and tapped a few of the buttons on the front of my harness. Suddenly, the dildo began throbbing with a deep rumble and another motor began vibrating against my nub under the harness.

"Holy shit," Alana hissed. "This thing is *way* better than my husband's cock. Whatever you're doing, it's driving me crazy. Fuck me harder, Jade. I'm getting close."

"So am I," I grunted, overwhelmed by the multiple sensations of fucking my neighbor from behind while simultaneously getting jilled on my clit. "Come with me baby. Let me feel you gushing all over my dick."

"Yes, Jade!" Alana cried. "Here it comes—I'm cumming!!"

Suddenly, I lost all sense of control as every ounce of my pent-up passion poured out of my body. As I began shuddering with intense contractions, I gushed my wetness out the sides of my harness down both sides of Alana's inner thighs. Feeling me cumming all over her, she wailed at the top of her lungs as her hips began shaking in spastic convulsions. I leaned over and squeezed her tits firmly with my hands as we both grunted in ecstatic union. When the two of us finished our long and intense climax and finally collapsed together on the floor, I noticed the rest of the girls lying beside us with silly grins on their faces.

This was one party none of us would soon forget.

VOLUME FOUR

SWEDISH SAUNA

1

I knew this trip was going to be different as soon as I stepped onto the plane. The flight attendants aboard my SAS flight to Stockholm were drop-dead gorgeous. Not just typical cute-stewardesses pretty, like top supermodel stunning. Every one of them was tall, slim, and *built*. With high cheekbones, full pouty lips, and steel-blue eyes, I felt like was like I was being transported to another *planet*, not another country. One where everybody had natural blonde hair, sexy figures, and movie-star looks.

As I streamed down the aisle with the other passengers, I couldn't stop staring at the crew as they greeted the travelers with perfect smiles and lilting European accents. Instantly smitten, I felt my skin beginning to moisten while I gawked at them like a star-struck colt. When a hunky male attendant in a tight blue uniform offered to help me lift my overstuffed carry-on bag into the overhead storage compartment, I stuttered like an infatuated schoolgirl.

"Can I help you with that madam?" he offered.

"Um, yes," I said, flushing unconsciously. "I guess I overpacked for such a short trip."

As he effortlessly lifted my bag into the bin, I watched his pec muscles bulging under his neatly pressed shirt, with my face mere inches away from his chest.

"How long will you be staying in Sweden?" he asked, flashing me a full set of pearly whites.

With his handsome face and tall muscular build, he looked like a dead-ringer for the Scandinavian actor Alexander Skarsgard.

"Just a couple of weeks," I muttered.

"You can't be too careful at this time of the year," he said. "Wintertime in Sweden can be quite chilly and the nights are very long. It's best to bundle up."

"Thank you," I said, smiling at him warmly.

"Enjoy your stay," he nodded before moving down the aisle to assist another passenger.

When I plopped down into my seat, I suddenly became conscious of how wet my panties had become in the short time I'd been on the plane. A slightly older woman sitting across the aisle from me glanced at the beads of perspiration on my forehead and smiled.

"He had the same effect on me," she grinned. "Do you think *everyone* in Sweden is this beautiful?"

"I don't know," I said, shaking my head. "But if so, this should be one hell of an interesting trip."

I pulled out my phone and pretended to text someone on the screen. I knew it was going to be a long flight overseas, and I didn't want another Chatty-Cathy burning up my ear the entire way. I didn't want to lose another moment soaking up the dazzling flight attendants as they walked up and down the aisle.

When the doors finally closed and the jet began to pull away from the gate, I was happy to have an unobstructed view of the pretty stewardesses from my perch at the back of the forward cabin. As the lead flight attendant provided instructions over the intercom system, her pretty assistant took up position at the front of the aisle and smiled at me. Normally, I ignored these boring safety demonstrations, burying my head in a newspaper or playing games on my phone. But on this flight, virtually every passenger in the first-class compartment sat upright in rapt attention, with all eyes on the model at the front of the room.

While the attendant demonstrated how to properly use the seat-belts and oxygen masks, I squeezed my legs together to quell my throbbing pussy. Beyond her perfect bone structure and pretty updo under her tight bellman's cap, her skin was absolutely flawless. Her creamy alabaster tone radiated a natural blush over her Nordic cheekbones, her ramrod-straight posture reinforcing the impression of watching a model on the catwalk. When she raised her arms to point out the location of the emergency exits, her full breasts pressed against the front of her blouse, showing off her Amazon-perfect physique.

Jesus, I thought, listening to myself audibly panting as I watched her go through the motions. *No wonder men joke about the Swedish Bikini Team as their ultimate fantasy. These people really are as gorgeous as the legend says.*

As I sat in my chair getting more and more turned on watching the sexy flight attendant, I felt like I had a front-row seat at a Paris fashion show. I had the blind fortune of checking out some of the most beautiful people on Earth from in my own personal viewing room. Even my first-class leather chair made it seem like I was sitting in my home studio watching an Ingmar Bergman movie. I was glad the window seat next to me hadn't been filled, as I squirmed between the armrests trying to give my aching clit some much-needed stim-ulation.

But as I began to fantasize about taking the sexy flight attendant into one of the lavatories for a mile-high fling, the demonstration abruptly ended and she took a seat facing me at the front of the cabin in preparation for takeoff. Soon after, the jets began to roar and I felt the pull of gravity push me back against my seat as the plane lifted off the runway. When the attendant made eye contact with me momen-tarily, I fantasized that it was *her* pressing against me instead of the pull of the aircraft.

As she politely glanced around the cabin, I couldn't take my eyes off her. Whenever our eyes met, I looked away, embarrassed at my invasion of her personal space. As the heat between my legs began to build and the dampness in my panties spread, I peered up at the seatbelt sign, impatient to go to the restroom to relieve my pent-up tension. Watching this sexy goddess had gotten me thoroughly worked up and I knew it wouldn't take much to get me off. Even though it wouldn't be as glamorous as the usual in-flight fantasy, I'd have my own fun envisioning the two of us intertwined in the close confines of the tight water closet.

But when the bell chimed signaling that we'd reached cruising altitude and could remove our seatbelts, I found myself wanting to stay in my seat when I saw her getting up to begin the meal service. As she moved down the aisle offering a choice of beverages, I leered at her firm ass whenever she leaned over to hand a glass to one of the passengers. I was happy to be seated in the last row of the first-class cabin, with the relative privacy of the partition separating me from the coach compartment.

While I pretended to flip through the inflight magazine resting on my lap, my right hand began to inch between my legs in desperate need of stimulation for the aching nub underneath my jeans. The closer the cute attendant got to my seat, the more excited I got caressing myself under my magazine. By the time she reached my row, my eyes had already glazed over as I needed all my strength to contain the pleasure beginning to consume my body.

"Champagne?" she said, turning to me with a tray filled with tall goblets.

"Um, yes, thank you," I stammered, gripping the sides of my magazine tightly with two hands.

When she leaned over to hand me the glass, I couldn't help staring at her ample breasts spilling out over the top of her tight vest. A silver name tag dangled from her blouse reading Elsa.

"Can I get you anything else?" she said, smiling at me as I blushed shyly.

"What else are you offering?" I asked, my mind racing ahead with fantasies of her jumping into my lap while I ravished her in my quiet little alcove.

"Coffee, tea, juice," she offered. "Or would you prefer another cocktail?"

There was only *one* kind of tail I was thinking about at this particular moment.

"This will be fine for now, thank you Elsa," I said, biting my lip at the temptation to flirt with her further.

"I'll return in a little while with your meal service," she said. "Would you like the salmon or the filet mignon?"

I smiled, happy that I'd chosen to fly first-class for a change. Not only was the food and service a notch above normal, but I had a far better view of the pretty flight attendants in the smaller confines of the forward cabin.

"I'll have the salmon, thank you," I said, fixing my gaze on her brilliant blue eyes.

When she began walking back to the front of the plane, my eyes locked again on her firm ass.

That's not the only thing I'd like to eat right now, I thought, imagining my face buried between her thighs while she sat facing me on the sink in the lavatory.

While I continued undressing her with my eyes, my clit throbbed painfully under my tight jeans. After a few more minutes of anguished frustration, I finally stood up and bee-lined my way to the washroom. When I opened the door next to Elsa working in the galley, she turned around and glanced down at my midsection. I smiled at her, then closed the door and looked at myself in the mirror in shock.

Was she just checking me out? I thought. *What would be the chances of getting her to join me in here? Maybe if I leave the door slightly ajar...*

I shook my head, realizing the absurdity of my fantasy.

These kinds of things only happen in Penthouse Forum letters. There's no way a professional flight attendant would risk this kind of impropriety while on duty.

As I started unzipping my jeans to free my burning jewel, I noticed they were wet in the front. Peering down in the mirror, I saw that a large wet spot had formed in the crotch.

"*Fuck!*" I cursed out loud. "*That's* why she was looking at me that way."

I blushed in embarrassment at being found out, wondering how many other passengers had used this hiding place for release after watching these vixens go about their work. But at this point, the stain on the front of my pants was the last thing I was worried about. Right now, I just needed to get off, and quickly. I pulled off my jeans and underwear and hung them on the back of the door, then placed my right foot on top of the vanity. My slit stretched open as my flaming clit protruded out of its hood.

Gawd how I'd like to grind my pussy against Elsa's face right now, I thought.

I washed my hands under the sink then thrust two fingers deep into my pussy as I began to fuck myself, watching my reflection in the mirror.

If Elsa could only see me now, I dreamed. I had a pretty good figure for a thirty-six-year-old woman, and my looks were nothing to sneeze at either. Would she be able to resist keeping her hands off me, watching me fuck myself like this mere inches away?

As I began to feel the pleasure rising within me, I started to moan, pretending that Elsa was peering back at me in the mirror instead of my own reflection. I was happy for the background drone of the jet engines so that no one could hear me.

"Fuck me, Elsa," I panted. "Rub your beautiful body against me while we grind our pussies together and enjoy our own inflight entertainment."

While I imagined Elsa moaning in my ear and rubbing her tits against mine, my climax suddenly washed over me like a tidal wave as I grunted and spasmed over the sink. With my fingers embedded deeply in my hole, I jerked my hand up firmly against my mound while I gushed all over my palm. I was glad that I'd had the foresight to remove my jeans completely, because by the time I finished cumming, I'd produced quite a puddle on the floor underneath me.

Damn—I needed that, I panted, nodding at my reflection in the mirror.

I grabbed a few towelettes from the dispenser and wiped the floor, then washed my hands thoroughly and put my clothes back on. Realizing that I'd be revealing the stain on the front of my jeans for the entire cabin to see on my return trip to my seat, I loosened my blouse and draped it over the front of my crotch. Thankfully, it hung just low enough to cover the wet spot without looking too conspicuous. Then I brushed my hair and reapplied my lipstick to make myself presentable and opened the door. Elsa was still working in the galley, and she smiled at me as her eyes drifted down my body.

Had my ruffled blouse given away what I was up to in the lavatory? I wondered. *Or had she heard my moans over the noise of the jet engines?* At this point I hardly cared, and I smiled back at her with a flush in my cheeks as I walked back to my seat.

For the next hour or so, the cabin was fairly busy with the movement of the two first-class flight attendants serving and collecting the main meal service. I made small talk with Elsa whenever she passed by my seat, introducing myself and sharing my plans while I stayed in Sweden. When I told her that I intended to get in some snowboarding during my stay, she told me about the best resorts to visit in the northern part of the country. I was tempted to invite her to join me on my excursion, but my shyness got the better of me.

When things settled down after the meal service, she took a seat for a brief rest in one of the jump seats next to the main door. As she opened a magazine, I took the opportunity to study her body from head to toe. Her legs were crossed while she read the magazine, and the swelling of her calf resting on her knee amplified the sexy curviness of her long legs. I could see her dark leggings running up the underside of her skirt and wondered if they were full-height pantyhose or mid-thigh stockings with garters. It didn't take long for me to begin fantasizing once again about fucking her as she sat quietly reading her magazine.

Only this time I wanted freer access to my pussy, where I could feel my slippery slit directly and rub my burning button without any impediments. I reached up and pressed the overhead call button, and Elsa looked up when she heard the chime. She peered down the aisle and noticing the light illuminated next to my console, she put down her magazine and walked toward me.

Damn, I thought to myself as I watched her glide down the aisle. *She even walks like a supermodel.* With her narrow foot placement down the cramped aisle, her hips swayed from side to side as her calves flexed with each step. I felt sorry disturbing her from her well-earned rest, but I needed one more thing from her.

"Yes, Jade," she said when she reached my seat. "What can I get you?"

"I was wondering if you had a blanket I could use to keep warm?" I said, peering up at her innocently. "It's a bit chilly in the cabin and I didn't bring a shawl in my carry-on bag."

"Yes, of course," she said. "I'll be back in a moment."

Elsa strolled back to the front of the cabin and opened a storage locker, pulling out plastic-covered packet. Then she walked back down the aisle and handed me the folded blanket.

"Was there anything else I can get to make your flight more comfortable?"

I paused for a moment raising an eyebrow, then shook my head.

"This should be fine for now," I said with a knowing smile. "I'm sure this will make the rest of my flight much more relaxing."

Little did she know what I *really* needed the blanket for. I just wanted some cover while I touched myself secretly in the privacy of my corner while I watched her from a distance.

"Just give me a ring if you need anything else," she said.

"I will, thank you Elsa."

As she began walking back up the aisle, I glanced at the woman sitting across the aisle from me and noticing that she had nodded off, I pulled my jeans and panties down below my knees. It felt exhila-rating to feel the cool gust of the jet breeze rushing up between my bare thighs. When Elsa returned to her seat, I glanced up at her and smiled, then she picked up her magazine and lowered her head.

Perfect, I thought. *You lose yourself in your little distraction while I lose myself in you as I get distracted doing other things.*

I snaked my right hand under the blanket and moistened the tips of my fingers with my slippery juices, then pulled them up and began circling my throbbing gland. Watching Elsa's pretty face while she read her magazine was the perfect aphrodisiac while I enjoyed myself under my blanket. As I rubbed my hard nub, I looked at her lips covered in clear gloss, imagining what it would feel like to have them surrounding my pearl. It didn't take long for me to start squirming in my seat as the pleasurable feelings began spreading throughout my body. Elsa peered up over the top of her magazine, and I looked away in embarrassment realizing she'd caught me staring at her once again. But when I glanced back at her, I noticed that she was still looking in my direction as she darted her eyes between my face and the bump in the blanket between my legs.

Did she sense what I was doing? I wondered. *Had I been too obvious in my amateur subterfuge?*

Either way, there was no way I was going to stop, because I'd gotten far too worked up to abandon my solo entertainment. As I returned her gaze, I slowly resumed rubbing my clit under the covering. At first, I did it in such a way that she'd have a hard time recognizing any suspicious movement. The last thing I needed was to get arrested for lewd or inappropriate behavior. I knew airlines had a low tolerance for disruptive passengers, and I had nightmares of being carted off the airplane in handcuffs in front of my fellow passengers upon landing.

But far from ignoring me or raising the alarm to her colleagues, Elsa seemed just as interested in what I was doing as I was in her. While she shifted her eyes between the magazine and the other passengers to distract attention from her watching me, I became bolder and bolder in my actions. I spread my legs wider apart and began to move my hand more quickly over my mound.

When it became obvious to Elsa what I was doing under my blanket, she lifted her leg and swung her thigh on top of her other knee. This time, I could see the curvature of her exposed thigh as her skirt hiked half way up her leg. While my hand began to move more forcefully under my blanket, I saw the muscles in Elsa's legs flexing rhythmically as she squeezed her legs together on her chair.

Is she stimulating herself while she watches me get off? I wondered.

Her quiet act of self-pleasure ratcheted up the intensity of my feelings even more, as I moved my other hand under the blanket and began to play with my sopping slit while I rubbed my bean with my other hand. Seeing that I was getting more worked up watching her at the front of the cabin seemed to increase Elsa's courage in lock-step, as the flexing action of her legs increased in speed and intensity. Recognizing that she was stimulating herself in full view of the rest of the cabin was an insane turn-on for me, and I thrust my fingers deep into my snatch, pummeling myself as I watched the flush on Elsa's face begin to spread down her neck onto the top of her chest.

I was aching for release, and when I saw her suddenly hunch over and pretend to cough as her body began to spasm, I gushed all over my hand, cumming hard for the second time during the flight. When she sat back up and glanced in my direction, I was still jerking in my seat with my mouth agape. She tried not to stare at me to avoid drawing attention from the other passengers, but she couldn't help flitting her eyes back toward me until I finally collapsed in my seat in delirious exhaustion.

For the rest of the flight, the two of us pretended like nothing had happened, continuing to carry on casual conversation while she attended to the needs of rest of the passengers. When we began to descend into Arlanda airport, I pulled myself together and collected my belongings in preparation for deplaning.

But by now, the stain in the front of my jeans had spread to the size of a grapefruit from the puddle I'd been sitting on, and I waited for the rest of the first-class passengers to disembark before rising from my seat. Holding my purse strategically over the front of my pants to hide the wet spot, I collected my bag from the overhead bin then made my way to the front exit door. Elsa was standing beside the exit wishing everyone well, and I paused for a moment before heading out onto the jetway.

"Thank you for such a memorable flight," I said, taking her hand and clasping it warmly between mine. "That was the most exceptional customer service I've ever experienced."

"The pleasure was all mine," Elsa smiled, placing her other hand over top of mine. "Enjoy your stay in our lovely country. Perhaps I'll see you on the return leg of your journey."

"I'll look forward to that," I said, realizing that I was holding up the rest of the passengers from exiting the plane. "Bye for now."

As our hands began to separate, Elsa pressed her fingers into the palm of my hand and I felt a strip of paper fall into my palm. I looked at her inquisitively, and she simply smiled and nodded. The moment I got through the jet bridge into the relative privacy of the main terminal, I stopped and unfolded the strip of paper she'd handed me.

Hope you enjoyed your inflight experience, the message read. *Drop me a line when you get settled in Stockholm. Perhaps we can enjoy a few more rides together on the slopes of the interior. Elsaflygirl@gmail.com*

I smiled a silly grin as I pulled my carry-on bag toward the exit door.

That wasn't the *only* kind of riding I had in mind for the remainder of my trip.

2

After I checked into my hotel room, I started up my laptop and opened a new email message. As my hands hovered over the keyboard, I pondered how best to respond to Elsa's invitation. Had she been thinking the same thing I was when she mentioned taking a few more 'rides' together? Was her choice of the words 'slopes of the interior' code for getting undressed and touching each other's naked bodies? Or was she just referring to snowboarding on the mountains of the north country?

Fuck it, I thought as I began to tap the keys. Either way, I wanted to see more of her—any way I could. We'd already shared an undeniably erotic moment together. There'd be plenty of other opportunities to get to know each other better during a few days of snowboarding together.

Hi Elsa, I typed.

Thank you for your lovely note. It was a pleasure meeting you on my flight to Stockholm, even if it was quicker than I hoped. I'd love to have a chance to get to know you better. Do you have some free time to do some snowboarding before your next flight? I'll be in Sweden for a week and I've got an open itinerary. Let me know if you'd like to get together,

Best wishes,

Jade.

For a few moments, I sat in front of my computer hoping she'd reply right away to my message. But after a few minutes, I realized how foolish it was of me to expect her to pause her normal routine just because we'd shared a passing moment on the transatlantic flight. I wondered how many *other* passengers had been equally obsessed by her and made similar passes. Surely, she'd have her choice of the most successful and prettiest travelers if she really wanted to strike up a more serious relationship.

I slammed my laptop shut and got up to distract myself from my single-minded infatuation. After all, I'd come to Sweden for a lot more reasons than just to meet new people. Between exploring the fjords, seeing the northern lights, and shopping the old city of Stockholm, there was plenty to do during my one-week stay. I'd even thought about staying one night at the famous ice hotel in Jukkasjarvi. But mostly I just wanted to recharge my batteries from my boring life in Chicago. I'd been flitting from one shallow relationship to another and needed a change. I figured the further I got away from home, the easier it would be for me to forget about my troubles. I hadn't planned on being gobsmacked by the most beautiful woman I'd seen in a long time.

After I unpacked my clothes and arranged my toiletries, I couldn't help checking my computer for new messages. To my surprise, I had a letter from Elsa marked only a few minutes after I'd sent my note. As I clicked to open the message, my stomach fluttered in excitement wondering what new adventures awaited me.

Jade, her message began.

How nice to hear from you so soon after our flight. I've been thinking of you too, and was wondering if you'd like to join me and a few friends for a little ski trip. My parents have a cabin near the resort town of Are, and I'm traveling there tomorrow with a couple of girls from the airline for a few days of R&R. The easiest way to get there is by train from the central station in Stockholm. There's a departure around 9 p.m. tonight that will get you in to the village early in the morning. If it's not too quick a turnaround for you, I can pick you up when you arrive and we'll all head out to the hill together. You're welcome to stay with us at my parents' place until you're scheduled to leave.

Looking forward to more adventures together,

Elsa

While I read the message, I could feel my heart beating in my chest as I imagined spending more time with the pretty stewardess. But now I'd have to share her with her friends, and I wondered if that would get in the way of our having some more intimate moments together. But she'd already demonstrated that she was attracted to women, and it didn't take long for me to imagine the bunch of us enjoying some quality après-ski time in the cosy confines of her alpine cabin. Besides, if the *girls* she was referring to were the other attendants on the flight from Chicago, the more the merrier. I'd have my very own fantasy bikini team to play with for a few days.

I quickly accepted her invitation, then packed up my things and checked out of the hotel, grabbing a cab to the downtown train station. I was surprised how packed it was for a Saturday evening, and after purchasing my ticket to Are, it took a while to get my bearings and find my way to the right departure track. When the train pulled up, I was impressed at how sleek and clean it looked. So far, I'd found everything about this country to be beautiful, polished, and efficient. Even my round-trip fare for the six-hundred-kilometer trip was thrifty, costing less than a hundred bucks.

When I stepped inside the train, I placed my snowboard gear and travel bag in the overhead rack then settled into a seat next to the window. Everything about the train was first-class, from the spotless upholstery and gleaming handrails to the crystal-clear panoramic windows. Even the *people* on the train looked stylish, dressed in fashionable parkas and fur-lined hats.

When the train began to exit the station, I peered outside the window and watched the passing streetscape flash by. I marveled at the pretty architecture of the multi-colored townhomes and plentiful canals running through the city. Within thirty minutes, the train was hurtling through the snowy forest of the interior, and I soon nodded off with my head resting against the glass.

Three hours later, I woke to the feeling of the chilly window pressing against my head, and I looked outside to see a strange glow moving in the night sky. Realizing this was the fabled northern lights I'd read so much about, I craned my neck to take in the eerie spectacle. The luminous bands swirled and morphed into ever-changing shapes and patterns, like a giant fluorescent ghost dancing in the sky. Now I understood why the indigenous people of the arctic gave such spiritual meaning to this supernatural light show. The swaying bands of color almost looked like a living organism, undulating in perpetual rhythm in the northern atmosphere.

There's another thing I can knock off my bucket list, I thought, staring up at the sky with my eyes agape in wonder.

But as the train continued north, the skies began to fill with clouds, and I checked my watch to see what time it was. The nights were over sixteen hours long at this latitude at this time of year, and I didn't want to arrive at my final destination unprepared. Even though it was approaching 8 a.m., it was still pitch-black outside and the train would be arriving into Are within thirty minutes. I went into the onboard lavatory to check my makeup and have a quick pee, then wrapped a scarf around my neck under my snow jacket, wondering if I'd prepared sufficiently for the cold Nordic weather.

When the train stopped, I gathered up my gear and headed for the station exit. Elsa hadn't been very specific about how we'd find one another at the train station, so when I got outside I stood on top of the steps surveying the parking area. There were a lot of passengers milling about with cars pulling up into the pick-up zone, so I pulled off my woolen cap and began waving in the general area of the logjam.

A few seconds later I heard a car horn beeping and a late-model Volvo SUV pulled up in front of me with the headlights flashing. The passenger window rolled down and a familiar face smiled at me, motioning for me to approach the car. The rear latch swung open and Elsa stepped out of the driver's seat waving back at me. I smiled at her and threw my board over my shoulder as I walked in their direction. When I got to the car, she gave me a big hug and threw my gear in the rear compartment on top of a bunch of other boots and snowboards.

"Did you have any trouble finding your way here?" she asked.

"No," I smiled. "It was pretty uneventful, other than the spectacular pyrotechnics in the evening sky."

"Ah yes," she said. "The aurora borealis. Was that the first time you'd seen the northern lights?"

"Yes—and it was even more beautiful than I imagined."

"We'll have lots more opportunities to view it over the next couple of nights from my cabin."

She opened the rear driver's side door and motioned me inside.

"But first, let's have a bit of fun on the slopes. I think you'll find the *daytime* views can be almost as pretty in this part of the country."

When I stepped inside the vehicle, two familiar-looking blonde girls turned toward me and smiled. I recognized both of them instantly as the other flight attendants on my inbound trip, and dressed in their pastel snowboard outfits they looked even prettier close-up.

"Do you remember Astrid and Inga from the flight?" Elsa said.

"Of course," I said, thinking I'd died and gone to heaven, surrounded by the three gorgeous women. "How could I forget?"

On the way from the station to the ski resort, we made small talk about my plans while in Sweden and what my life was like back in Chicago. The girls said they traveled there frequently, and I immediately returned the invitation, inviting them to stay with me the next time they were in town. But the whole conversation was a blur as I kept flitting my eyes between the three striking Vikings sitting next to me in the car.

When we got to the ski hill, we all carried our gear up to the lodge then went inside for a quick breakfast and coffee. The girls ordered cereal composed of muesli, fermented milk, and strawberries, and I followed along, trying to sample the local cuisine. It wasn't as bad as it sounded, and I soon gobbled down the crunchy yogurt-tasting concoction on my empty stomach. Then we wolfed down some strong coffee and went downstairs to the locker room to change into our snowboard gear. The three girls all seemed quite adapt at getting into their heavy boots, and when they pulled their goggles over their toques in preparation to exit the cabin a couple of minutes ahead of me, I shook my head in wonderment.

"You girls look like you've done this a few times before," I said, gazing up at their pretty two-piece parkas.

Elsa smiled, kneeling down to help me lace up my boots.

"There's not a lot to do during long winters here in the hinterland," she said. "It's pretty much a choice between hockey or snow skiing. And the airline frowns upon our taking part in contact sports. Something about keeping ourselves in top condition for our guests."

"I can see why," I said, peering at the Swedish beauties. "I wouldn't want to mess with perfection either if I had your looks."

"You know," Elsa said, holding a hand out to help me off the bench. "With your fair skin and light hair, you could easily pass for a Swede too. And I think you're selling yourself short. You're just as pretty as any Scandinavian girl. Speaking of, let's get out there while we still have good light. The rides close in a few hours and it looks like we've had some good powder overnight."

When we got outside, the girls snapped on their boards then shuffled their hips forward as they began to glide to the base of the nearest lift. When we neared the front of the line, we positioned ourselves four abreast and sat down on the wide chair as it swung around to pick us up. As it picked up momentum and lifted us off the ground, my pussy pulsed in excitement feeling the hips of the other girls pressing up against my sides.

"So what brings you to Sweden?" Astrid asked, puffing a cloud of condensed air into the chilly breeze as she spoke.

"Besides the beautiful people and the gorgeous scenery?" I said, peering out over the mountainous landscape. "I guess I was just looking for something new. I was getting kind of bored with my usual routine in Chicago. It's been a while since I've been on a trip outside the country."

"Well if you're looking for something different," Inga said, smiling at the other girls. "Stick with us. We'll be happy to introduce you to some of our more interesting Swedish customs. The après-ski scene can be just as much fun as the daytime opportunities."

Elsa noticed my hands gripping the safety bar in front of me tightly as I shivered under my light snowboard ensemble.

"Are you warm enough?" she said, placing her mittens over mine on the bar. "I noticed you weren't wearing as many layers as the rest of us under that thin parka."

"I'm used to dressing for the mild midwestern winters back home. I guess I wasn't quite ready for the temperatures up here."

"You'll warm up once we get out on the slopes," she said. "All you need is a little exercise to get the blood flowing."

She peered forward as our chair neared the top of the mountain.

"What kind of trails do you like to take? How experienced a snowboarder are you?"

"I don't get out as often as I'd like," I said, glancing down the steep slope underneath our lift. "I used to be pretty decent when I was younger, but it's been a couple of years since I've hit the slopes. Maybe something intermediate to start?"

"No problem," Elsa said. "Just head to the left when we get off the lift. We can start out on the blue trail. It's wide and gently sloping, with lots of room for us to carve wide unobstructed turns."

When the chair reached the crest of the hill, we all pushed off while I struggled to stay balanced as it thrust me forward. The other girls seemed far more composed and confident, shifting their weight expertly backwards as they dug their edges into the soft corn while I wobbled unsteadily, trying to keep my board from getting away from me.

"Ready?" Elsa said, flashing me a brilliant smile.

"I think so," I hesitated.

Seconds later, the girls pointed their boards down the hill and began carving up the light powder in tight serpentine patterns, three abreast. I watched them for a few moments, marveling at how effortless they made it seem, but also how pretty their tight asses looked twisting and swaying as they kicked up light sprays of powder, schussing their way down the meandering slope. Not wanting to get left too far behind, I shifted my weight forward and tentatively pointed my board on a diagonal line across the slope.

At first, I was reluctant to commit myself fully into the fall line, but as I began to shift my weight forward and back on my board, I was pleasantly surprised by how easy I could turn in the freshly fallen snow. Before long, I was carving figure eight patterns overtop the trails left by the other girls and smiling with a giant grin as I began to find my groove. About halfway down the hill, I noticed the they'd pulled up on a flat section of the slope and I skidded to a halt a few feet in front of them.

"*Damn*, Jade," Elsa said as I huffed a stream of fog into the cold air, trying to recover my breath. "You know how to *ride*, girl. That's some pretty sweet carving you were doing down the trail. We're going to have to step up our game to keep up with you."

"Hardly," I smiled. "You're the ones making it look easy. I'm already starting to feel the burn in my legs. You might need to give me a couple of days to ease into this, or else I might need a wheelchair to get back onto the plane for the ride back. Something tells me you guys have had a bit more practice at this than me."

"Maybe," Elsa said. "But you sure aren't any slouch. Why don't you go first this time and we'll follow. Show us your best Lindsey Vonn moves."

I thought it ironic that they'd likened me to the pretty American downhill champion who'd recently turned the European circuit on its ear.

"I'm not *that* good," I said. "I'll just be happy if I can make it down the rest of the way without wiping out."

This time I flipped my board forward and headed straight down the fall line, rapidly picking up speed as I arched my body from side to side, reveling in the soft champagne powder of the Swedish resort. When I got to the bottom of the hill and stopped at the base of the lift, the three other girls followed close behind and skidded to a stop beside me.

"It looks like you've found your legs," Elsa said. "You can carve, girl. I was admiring your form all the way down."

"Are you referring to my ski technique or my skimpy little outfit?" I smiled.

"Both. I had a hard time staying on the course with such a pretty distraction in front of me."

"Glad I was able to keep you distracted," I smiled. "I'm hoping there'll be lots of other opportunities to divert your attention over the next couple of days."

The four of us spent the next couple of hours carving the hills, taking increasingly steep and exciting trails before we decided we need a rest. When we stopped near the bottom of one of the trails, Elsa looked over toward me and smiled in a heavy plume of mist.

"Are you ready for some fika?" she said.

Not knowing exactly what that was, but sounding pretty close to fucking, I nodded eagerly, happy to have a different kind of alonetime with the girls.

"Let's head into the lodge," Elsa said. "I don't know about you guys, but I could eat a moose after a hard morning of riding."

"Count me in," Astrid said.

"I could use a warm cup of coffee right about now," Inga nodded.

"Is that what fika is?" I said, pinching my eyebrows in disappointment.

"Yes," Elsa said. "In Sweden, coffeetime is more of a social gathering opportunity than just an excuse to get charged up on caffeine. Let's go inside and rest up for a bit while we get warmed up. We don't want to turn your body into rubber on the first day."

We trudged into the lodge and found an open spot next to a large wood-burning fireplace. As the girls began to take off their heavy parkas and outerwear, I couldn't stop scanning their shapely figures in their tight, form-fitting sweaters. The cute reindeer motifs reminded me of Pippi Longstocking, but their swelling breasts and hourglass figures reminded me more of that other Swedish meme. There was something about the warmth of the roaring fire and the sweat dripping down the back of my neck from the exertion on the slopes that was quickly getting me worked up. As I continued undressing the girls with my eyes, my mind began to wander to the possible après-ski activities that Elsa had mentioned.

"Shall we get a bite to eat?" she said, catching me eyeing up her body.

"Absolutely," I said, trying to quell my churning insides. My stomach wasn't the *only* body part that needed attention right now. I needed a distraction quickly before I peeled off their clothes right then and there and jumped their bodies in my mind's imagination.

As we strolled up to the food line, I once again followed the girls' lead. Everybody was ordering hot pea soup or oven-cooked pancakes with ligonberry jam and maple syrup. But when it came time to order coffee, they all looked at me with a strange expression when I ordered a latte with extra cream and sugar.

"What?" I said, looking at the girls with a puzzled expression. "You guys are looking at me like I just ordered *antifreeze*."

"We don't put all that extra stuff in our coffee in Sweden," Elsa said. "We like to take it straight-up, where we can enjoy its natural goodness."

"Mmm, I get that," I said, glancing at her shapely ass in her tight leggings. "Straight up it is."

When we returned to our table next to the fire, I was surprised how good the pancakes and soup tasted. I was so used to the typical American brunch of bacon and eggs that I'd almost forgotten about the pleasures of a foreign diet. Even the plain coffee tasted unusually good, as I savored the natural flavor of the north African bean.

While we made small talk about our favorite trails at the resort, I couldn't help staring at the girls' shapely figures in their tight sweaters as their chests expanded and contracted while they ate their food. The orange flames from the fireplace cast a warm glow on their faces, accenting their natural beauty. By the time we'd finished our meal, my entire body was burning and flushed in excitement.

"So what do you guys do for fun after playing on the hills all day?" I said, hoping to plant the seeds for some more adventurous après-ski activities.

Elsa looked at her friends for a moment then peered at me with a devilish grin.

"Have you ever participated in a polar bear plunge?" she asked.

"Isn't that where people jump into freezing cold water in the middle of winter?" I said, shaking my head in bewilderment. "Isn't that kind of painful and dangerous?"

"Not the way we do it. We only stay in for a short time then head into the sauna to warm up. It's actually quite refreshing. After a hard day of snowboarding, the cold water actually reduces muscle inflammation and speeds up your recovery time."

"Do you guys wear some kind of special insulation?" I said, not quite buying Elsa's dubious explanation.

"Actually, the best way to do it is in the nude. The less clothing, the better. You don't want any cold clothing clinging to you when you get out of the water. We'll have terrycloth robes ready for you to warm up quickly. But the best part about it is the sauna afterward. Feeling the warm steam all over your newly cleansed skin is absolutely heavenly. It's is a tradition we Swedes have been practicing for centuries."

The idea of seeing the three pretty flight attendants in the buff quickly eliminated my concerns about the discomfort of the procedure. It actually sounded like a lot of fun, and my mind was already racing ahead to all the possibilities once we got in the sauna.

"When in Sweden..." I smiled, cocking my head playfully. "You guys certainly aren't holding back giving me the full immersion experience. I'm eager to learn *all* about your special customs."

"Good," Elsa said, reaching down to lace up her boots. "Let's get back out on the slopes while we've still got some good light. It'll turn dark in a couple of hours and we haven't even tried the most challenging trails."

I smiled nervously, feeling the burn in my thighs when I stood to zip up my jacket.

Hopefully the *rest* of my body will still be able to function by the time these girls are ready to stop torturing me, I thought.

3

───────

By three o'clock, the shadows were beginning to lengthen over the mountain, and the four of us headed back into the lodge to collect our belongings. I was actually looking forward to the dip in the cold water to help relieve my aching muscles. As we drove through the dense forest on the way to Elsa's cabin, I marveled at the natural beauty of the Scandinavian landscape. Heavy pillows of snow hung over the roofs of quaint chalets nestled among the tall evergreen trees, like icing on gingerbread houses. The woods got thicker and thicker, until we emerged onto a clearing with a small wooden cabin at the edge of an ice-covered lake.

"Here we are," Elsa said, pulling her car up next to a broad porch at the front of the structure. The setting reminded me of a prototypical arctic winter scene, like something out of a Christmas fairy tale.

"Let's go inside and get the fireplace going," she said. "You'll need to get warmed up before taking a dip in the lake."

When we stepped through the front door, I was surprised how cold the cabin was as I rubbed my hands over my shoulders trying to increase the circulation.

"Sorry about the chilly temperature," Elsa said. "We normally keep the furnace set just high enough to keep the pipes from freezing." She nodded toward a giant stone fireplace with tall stacks of wood framing the opening. "We prefer to heat our houses the natural way. There's nothing like the sound and smell of freshly cut birch cackling in the open hearth."

She kneeled down in front of the fireplace and rolled some newspaper into little balls then placed some kindling over top of them and struck a match. The material quickly burst into flame, and as she stacked the silver logs over the iron grate, the fire soon began roaring, throwing pretty sparks against the safety screen.

"*That's* what I'm talking about," I said, taking a seat on the mantle next to the fire, rubbing my cold fingers together.

"Can I get you something to drink while you warm up?" Elsa said. "Maybe a hot chocolate or a black coffee?"

"If it's not against the rules trying something a little sweet," I smiled. "A hot chocolate would be lovely."

Elsa disappeared into the kitchen and reemerged a few minutes later with a platter holding four steaming cups. She handed one to each of us, then the girls sat down on heavy armchairs facing me. I could feel my cheeks begin to flush as I gazed at them with the orange glow from the fire dancing over their pretty faces.

"So what do you think of our country so far?" Elsa said.

"It's a little chillier than I imagined," I said, clasping my mug between my palms to warm up my still-tingling hands. "But everything about it certainly is beautiful."

"We'll get you warmed up soon enough," she smiled. "Would you like a little tour of my chalet? We've got the place all to ourselves for the next few days, and you'll need to know where to find the water closet and other amenities. Besides, I need to stoke the coals in the sauna to heat it up in preparation for our polar bear plunge."

"Oh yeah," I said, huddling closer to the fire. "I'd almost forgotten about that."

As I followed Elsa through the different rooms of the cabin, I was struck by how small the place was. With only two bedrooms and one washroom, I wondered how four girls would comfortably share the space for more than a few days. But I hesitated asking about the sleeping arrangements, hoping we'd be able to at least double-up in the small space. I was already beginning to plan how I'd nestle up against Elsa on the pretense of getting warm as a prelude to more intimate exploration.

When we reached the back of the cabin, Elsa opened a heavy door and the smoky scent of fresh cedar filled my nostrils as I peered into a large wood-paneled room. Every surface of the interior was lined in reddish-brown planks of wood, with wraparound wooden benches on two levels surrounding a small metal stove topped with gray rocks.

"Wow," I said, inhaling the smoky scent. "This room is even bigger than the bedrooms. You must spend a lot of time in here."

"Having a daily sauna is like a spiritual experience for us Swedes," Elsa nodded. "It's part of our DNA. There's no better way to relax and wind down after a busy day."

She stepped toward the little stove and placed a large ladle into a wooden bucket of water. As she spilled the liquid gently over the glowing rocks, a hot steam began to fill the room with a pleasant eucalyptus aroma.

"That's an interesting way to warm up a room," I said, my heart racing at the thought of soon lying in the heavenly space next to the three beauties.

"Radiant heat is the cleanest type of heat," Elsa nodded. "Plus, the humidity does wonders for cleaning out your lungs and your pores. You'll feel like a new woman after spending a couple of hours in here."

"I can imagine," I said, beginning to feel my pussy perspire at the thought.

"Are you ready for a bracing swim first?" Elsa said, flashing me a sly grin.

"I guess so," I murmured, preferring to stay in the comfortable and aromatic environment of the steam room.

"Let's get changed out of our outerwear," she said, opening an adjacent closet. "I've got some heavy robes to keep you warm before and after the swim."

We all returned to the living room, where the three girls began to disrobe. I hesitated at first, nervous to reveal my naked body among a group of strangers. But as they peeled off their layers showing more and more skin, I slowly began to undress. Their firm breasts bounced on their chests as they pulled off their undershirts and I couldn't help gasping when they finally removed all their clothes. All three of them had creamy pale skin and Playmate-perfect figures. With nary a hair to be found anywhere on their bodies below their flowing blonde locks, my pussy pulsed in excitement as I stared at them unashamedly.

"Jesus," I said, shaking my head in amazement. "Is *everybody* in Sweden in this good shape? You guys all look like somebody straight out of a beer commercial."

"Yeah—we get that Swedish Bikini Team thing all the time," Elsa said, shaking her head. "I'm not sure Budweiser did us any favors creating that image of Scandinavian girls for North American consumption."

She gave my body a quick going over as I pulled off the last of my underclothes.

"But you're no slouch either, Jade. With your blonde locks and athletic figure, you could pass for a Swedish girl any day."

I stood awkwardly facing the three girls, feeling the heat of the nearby fire burning the back my naked body.

"I'm just happy to be mentioned in the same *sentence* with you guys, let alone be thought of as one of your countrymen," I said, hoping to deflect everyone's attention from my naked figure. "Are we going to do this or what?"

"Of course," Elsa said, handing out terrycloth robes and slippers to each of us. "But be careful as you walk down the path toward the water. There's plenty of ice, and the rocks are quite slippery. You might want to hold my hand as you make your way over the flagstones."

We all put on our gowns, then Elsa opened the front door as I felt a rush of cold air enter the cabin.

"Come on, scaredy-cat," she said, holding out her arm for me. "We don't want to let the cabin get cold again. Let's take a dip before you lose your nerve."

I wrinkled my forehead, then took Elsa's hand as the four of us scampered down the frozen flagstone path to a small dock extending out over the water. When we got to the end of pier, I noticed a ten-foot-diameter hole cut into the ice covering of the pond and I looked at Elsa with an incredulous expression.

"You want me to go in *there*?" I said with my eyes agape.

"Just for a few moments," she said. "I promise you'll enjoy it. There's nothing so invigorating as a brief plunge into freezing-cold water to charge up your adrenaline. Are you ready?"

"I don't know..." I said, pulling back on Elsa's hand.

Suddenly, Astrid and Inga threw off their robes and jumped into the black pool, emerging from the frigid surface hollering in delight.

"Come on in, Jade," Inga said, flinging her wet hair behind her head. "The water's lovely. Come experience the crystal-clear water of our natural habitat."

"Natural habitat?" I scoffed. "Maybe for a *polar bear*."

Elsa turned to face me and squeezed my hand.

"Come on Jade, you're just torturing yourself standing out here in the cold air. We'll jump in together and it'll be over before you know it. Then we can all get nice and cozy in the warm sauna."

There was something about the way she said *nice and cozy* that encouraged me to get this over with.

"Ready?" she said, dropping her robe onto the dock.

I looked at her sexy body shining in the bright moonlight and pulled off my frock.

"One–two–THREE!" she shouted, then she leaped off the dock pulling me into the pitch-black lake.

It took a moment to register the feeling of the cold water surrounding my body as my mind was still in shock at the audacity of what we were doing. But within seconds, I could feel the painful burn of the freezing depths as my teeth began to clatter while I treaded water.

"Isn't it *fabulous*?" Elsa said, smiling at me with a big toothy grin.

"Ye-yes," I stuttered, trying to block out the numb feeling rapidly spreading over my body. "That's one thing you could call it."

"Look, up at the sky," she said, peering upward. "The northern lights are even more beautiful this far away from the city."

"It's stunning," I said, recognizing the swirling green clouds. "But I think I could appreciate it better dressed up in a warm sweater from your front porch with a warm cup of coffee resting on my lap."

"Okay," Elsa nodded. "I think we've exposed you long enough to the natural elements for one night. Let's get out of here and warmed up."

She swam to the front of the dock and climbed up a small wooden ladder then held out her hand to me as she bent down over the edge.

"Give me your hand so you don't slip getting up."

As I kicked my way to the ladder and placed my hands on the rungs, I could feel my muscles shaking as I tried to pull myself up. Elsa grabbed one of my hands and lurched me out of the water, then wrapped one of the robes around my shivering body. As she held me close trying to share her body heat, I watched the other two girls emerge from the pool with beads of water running over their sexy figures. Their areolas contracted with deep goose bumps as their hard nipples extended out from their breasts almost a full inch. For a moment, I forgot that I was standing near-naked in subfreezing temperatures soaking wet while I admired their sexy bodies.

"Come on," Elsa said. "Let's get back into the cabin and warm up in the sauna. I think you're ready for a new kind of Swedish experience."

The four of us scurried up the path, then Elsa opened the front door and we scampered over the hardwood floor into the sauna. While Elsa poured three ladles of water over the steaming coals, the room soon filled with the soothing sensation of the humid heat. I sat down next to the stove, with the other three girls sitting on the two levels directly opposite me.

"There," Elsa purred. "Doesn't that feel a little better?"

"Yes," I said. "But not enough to take off my clothes quite yet. I'm still warming up in this nice cozy robe."

"Feel free to keep it on for a little longer," Elsa said. "But we normally like to take our saunas in the nude. Soon you'll begin to sweat and you'll want to give your pores a chance to open up and let your body cleanse yourself."

As if on cue, Astrid and Inga unfastened their belts and pulled their robes open, revealing their glistening breasts.

"Yes," I panted. "I want to experience *everything* here in Sweden the same way you native girls do."

"You know," Elsa smiled. "I kind of like watching you covered up. It reminds me of our little affair on the plane."

"Oh?" I said. "You remember that still?"

"How could I forget?" Elsa grinned. "That was the most interesting flight I've had in a long time."

"You seemed to be enjoying yourself almost as much as I was."

"I have a little secret to confess," she said. "I had a little help of my own while I watched you."

"Really?" I said, pinching my eyebrows together in confusion. "I saw you flexing your thighs, but–"

"There was a little more than that going on. I had something *inside* while I was rubbing myself."

"Inside?"

"Ben-wa balls. Have you ever tried those before?"

"I've heard of them but never tried it. How do they work?"

"You gently rock your hips or squeeze your legs together, and they roll around inside your pussy providing a very erotic sensation. It's quite an exquisite feeling. I have them inside me right now."

"*You do?*" I said, widening my eyes in surprise. "How do you keep them from falling out?"

"It's not hard to keep them in using your Kegel muscles. In fact, it's considered a good way to exercise those muscles to maintain optimal sexual function."

Elsa paused for a moment, as she began to spread her legs apart.

"Can you do me a favor and play with yourself under your robe while I replay our little erotic encounter on the plane?"

"*Hell* yes," I said, happy to see that Elsa and the other girls were just as interested as I was moving our relationship to the next level of intimacy.

As I slipped my hand under my robe, I felt my still cold and clammy skin over the front of my hairless mound. But as I moved my fingers over my slit, I felt my warm natural juices beginning to lubricate my vulva.

"Mmm," I purred, watching Astrid and Inga spread their legs further apart as they watched me. "I *like* seeing you in your natural habitat."

"Yes," Elsa groaned, rocking her hips gently on the wooden bench. "You're very pretty, Jade. I've been dreaming about watching you up close ever since our flight ended."

"I was so happy when I read your note," I smiled. "I've pleasured myself many times replaying that moment over and over."

"As have I," Elsa said, rubbing her thighs together as she opened her robe wider for me to see her juggling tits. "And I wasn't the *only* one who enjoyed that memory," she said motioning to the other girls sitting on the bench beside her.

Astrid and Inga nodded as they moved their hands between their legs and began to circle their nubs.

"You *told* them?" I said, feigning surprise.

"Of course. We share everything together. You're not the *only* one who likes a little play time between girls every now and then."

I smiled at the revelation that they were all bisexual like me.

"It looks like the only person missing from your troop is the hot flight attendant who reminds me of Tarzan," I said

"You mean *Erik*?" Elsa said. "He's quite a dish to be sure, but I think he prefers to bat for the other team as much as we do."

"You mean he's gay?" I said. "What a shame. I was undressing him on the plane almost as much as I was you girls."

"Not to worry," Elsa smiled. "I'm pretty sure between the three of us that we'll be able to keep you properly entertained during your stay."

"I hope so," I panted, watching Astrid and Inga place their fingers inside their pussies while they jilled themselves watching me play with myself.

"Open your robe now," Elsa ordered. "Let me see exactly what you were doing under that blanket on the plane. I want to watch your pretty body while you pleasure yourself. It's just us girls this time and nobody else is watching."

I didn't need any more encouragement as I began to feel the pleasurable sensations spreading throughout my body. The rising steam from the coal stove had increased the room temperature to well over one hundred degrees and I didn't need any more excuses to fully disrobe. I took my gown off my shoulders and threw it on the bench beside me and spread my legs wide apart to let the girls see my glistening lips.

"Yes," Elsa said. "Show us what you were doing with your fingers under that blanket."

By now, I was burning up inside from the rising passion as I watched the three goddesses touching themselves while they watched me. I plunged my middle two fingers into my snatch and pulled my palm against my throbbing button, stroking myself with increasing intensity as the three women writhed on the wooded benches in front of me. Elsa spread her legs further apart, rocking her hips forward and back while she rubbed her clit in tight little circles.

"Yes, Jade," she purred. "Fuck that sweet pussy with your pretty fingers. I want to watch your body heaving and shaking again when you come."

"Damn, Elsa," I said, feeling the wall of pleasure rapidly building inside my body. "This is a feast for my eyes. I'm going to come soon."

"Yes, my pretty American," she said. "Let us watch you satisfy yourself while we pleasure our bodies. I'm close too."

As I watched the three beauties rocking their bodies on the warm planks, I felt my body fall over the precipice as I clamped down over my fingers, hunching over in a series of rhythmic spasms. With the pressure built up inside my pussy from my fingers damming the flow of my juices, I pulled my fingers out of my hole and began spraying long streams of fluid over the steaming wooden floor. Seeing me squirting my juices while racked in pleasure soon pushed the other girls over the edge, and within seconds all four of us were shaking and groaning in the steamy fog of the sauna.

"Now I see why you were covering yourself up when you left the plane," Elsa sighed when she came down from her climax. "That's one part of the experience I definitely missed. You are one talented and sexy lady, Jade."

"Not nearly as sexy as the three of you," I said, catching my breath. "That was the hottest show I've seen in a long time."

"I have to agree," Elsa smiled, peering at her colleagues. "What do you think girls? Is this the sexiest passenger we've ever had on our transatlantic flight?"

"Definitely," Astrid nodded. "I've seen a lot of fuckable passengers in my day, but nobody I've wanted to get down and dirty with as much as this one."

"And we're just getting started," Elsa grinned. "There's so many other ways we can have fun together now that we're free of all the limitations on the plane. What's your ultimate fantasy, Jade? What would you like to do now that you have the three of us all to yourself?"

"Oh my God," I said, realizing all my dreams were about to come true. "My mind is racing with so many possibilities right now. But honestly, I'd just like to watch you three do your thing together. This is the like the ultimate erotic video, watching three gorgeous girls touching each other. I'll be happy to get in on the action soon enough. For now, let me just soak up your fabulous figures a little longer while I watch you get a little more interactive."

Elsa smiled as she peered over at Astrid and Inga.

"What do you say, girls? Shall we indulge our guest in her little fantasy?"

"I thought she'd never ask," Inga smiled, shifting her body closer to Elsa.

"If you're just going to *watch*," Elsa said, pinching a little string between her legs and pulling two glistening chrome balls out of her slit. "Would you like to try my little toy? I think you might find it makes for a more engaging experience."

"Absolutely," I said, raising my eyebrows as I peered at the intriguing balls.

Elsa stood up and walked across the floor then handed me the slippery orbs. I could smell the musk of her scent on the globes and I looked up at her, grinning a broad smile.

"Just be sure to leave some of the string hanging out your opening," she said. "They can get pretty far up inside you in the heat of the moment and you don't want to lose them up there. Once you place them inside, you'll find plenty of ways to stimulate yourself. Enjoy."

Elsa returned to the other side of the room, sitting on the upper bunk while Astrid stood on the lower bench facing her with her back toward me. As she lowered her face toward Elsa's pussy, Inga sat between her legs and tilted her head up as Astrid planted her mound over her chin. Within seconds, all three girls were rolling their hips in a three-way ménage as they began to grunt and moan in unison.

Watching them pleasuring themselves just a few feet in front of me soon got my juices flowing again as I awkwardly pressed the two chrome balls into my slit. They slipped inside easier than I imagined, but it felt unusual to have such a strangely shaped object inside me other than the usual dildos and vibrators I was accustomed to.

But as I began to rock my hips slowly on the bench, I could feel them sliding forward and back against the walls of my pussy, and I soon began to mew and groan along with the other girls. It didn't take long for me to get comfortable with the pleasurable feeling of the slippery balls stroking the walls of my pussy, and when I placed my fingers against my dripping clit, I felt a jolt of electricity running through me.

This is a little different, I thought. *Why haven't I tried this before?*

Now I understood why Elsa brought them with her wherever she flew. With their unobtrusive form factor and concealed placement, no one would be any the wiser as she went about her duties receiving gentle, sensuous stimulation whenever she moved.

As I watched Elsa spread her legs wide apart and Astrid humping Inga's face while they ate each other out, I began to rock my hips faster and faster watching the girls bucking and moaning in front of me. With Inga's legs splayed far apart as she rubbed her bald pussy with her glistening fingers, and seeing the base of her chin planted firmly against Astrid's mound, watching the three girls fucking themselves in the superheated environment of the aromatic sauna was the most erotic thing I'd seen in a long time.

When Elsa placed her hands beside Astrid's head and pulled her face harder against her pussy as she locked eyes on me, I suddenly felt a surge of pleasure engulfing me. With our mouths yawning wider and wider apart in shared ecstasy, I couldn't hold back any longer.

"Oh *fuckkk,*" I groaned in pleasure, my body beginning to shake once again in another intense orgasm. I could feel the Ben-wa balls rolling around inside as my pussy walls contracting rhythmically against them, sending me into new paroxysms of pleasure.

Watching me shaking uncontrollably on the steamy wooden planks seemed to bring Elsa to a new level of pleasure, and soon she also began jerking spasmodically as she held Astrid's face tightly against her pussy. Like a chain reaction, Astrid suddenly became weak at the knees as she slumped forward against Inga's chin with her buttocks shaking like a bowl of water. Feeling Astrid coming all over her face, Inga raised her hips off the bench and began flapping her thighs in and out in mutual ecstasy. Realizing that all three girls were coming together took me to another level, and within seconds I was having my third powerful orgasm of the afternoon.

After we all come down from our climaxes, I suddenly became aware of the ache in my quads from my hard day of snowboarding. I'd been so lost in the moment watching the other girls having fun and pleasuring myself that I'd forgotten I'd just had the most intense exercise in months.

I'll have to take it easier on the slopes tomorrow, I thought, *if I'm going to keep up with these girls and enjoy some more off-piste action.* The après-ski experience had been even more exciting and adventurous than the vigorous snowboarding exercise. I wanted to save myself for the next step in my Swedish immersion.

4

Over the course of the next few days, Elsa, Inga, Astrid and I made love many more times between our snowboarding, polar plunge, and sauna escapades. By the end of the week, I'd experienced every erotic entanglement with the three girls that I'd fantasized about on my initial flight to Sweden. When it finally came time to say our goodbyes, I was sad to leave but thrilled to have had the opportunity to spend so much quality time with the three Scandinavian beauties.

As the four of us drove back to Stockholm in preparation for my return flight to Chicago, we talked about reconnecting stateside, but I never expected to see the girls again. We'd had our moment of glory together, and that was enough for me. I'd cherish the experience forever and carry enough memories to keep me entertained for quite some time into the future.

But I still had one last flight with the girls, and I planned to make the best of it. Elsa and I had talked over the last couple of days about how we might be able to arrange a *real* mile-high liaison, and my body was tingling all over in anticipation of the trip. After I passed through airport security and collected my boarding pass, I smiled at Elsa and Astrid as I boarded the plane and took my seat near the back of the first-class cabin. The same woman I'd met on my inbound flight was sitting across the aisle from me again, and I smiled politely before pretending to check my email messages.

While the rest of the passengers shuffled onto the plane, I tried to keep myself distracted reading a magazine while I squirmed uncomfortably in my seat. Watching Elsa do the safety demonstration drove me crazy knowing she was receiving internal stimulation the whole time from her Ben-wa balls. I cursed myself for not remembering to buy some of my own to keep me entertained during the long flight.

But when the demonstration was over and the girls took their seats in preparation for take-off, Elsa winked at me, giving me a sly smile. Within thirty minutes, we reached cruising altitude and Astrid and Elsa began delivering the meal service. It was difficult restraining myself from interacting with the girls in a more familiar manner, but I continued playing the role of naive first-time traveler to maintain their professional demeanor. Besides, I knew that very soon we'd be able to dispense with the charade and have one last chance at resuming our special relationship.

When the meal service was over, Elsa and Astrid seemed more generous than usual offering the passengers their choice of alcoholic beverage. Before long, most of the early-morning travelers had nodded off in their seats from the combined effects of full stomachs and the alcohol-induced sedative. The girls took their seats at the front of the cabin for a brief rest, and after briefly scanning the attentiveness of the passengers, Elsa nodded toward me and tilted her head in the direction of the forward lavatory.

I carefully glanced around the cabin and when I saw that everybody was either sleeping or absorbed in their reading material, I rose from my seat and slowly made my way up the aisle. As I opened the door to the lavatory, I smiled at the two flight attendants and they winked back at me. When I closed the door behind me, my heart began racing a million miles an hour thinking about what we were about to do. Whether it was from the danger of being exposed or from the excitement of soon reconnecting with my Swedish lovers, I wasn't sure. But either way, my panties were already soaked from the rush.

It seemed to take forever for Elsa to join me in the lavatory, and after a few minutes I began to wonder if some of the passengers had woken up or requested additional aid. Not knowing what to do with myself, I began to disrobe and hung my clothes on the peg over the door. Looking at my fully naked body in the mirror, I began to play with myself imagining her touching me in the private cubicle. Just as I was about to come remembering the sight of the three sexy stewardesses in the sauna, suddenly the door swung open and Elsa stepped inside. She looked at me hunched over the sink with my hands between my legs and smiled as she shut the door quietly behind her.

"It looks like you've gotten started without me," she said. "That's my girl. We won't have too much time to do this while Astrid is keeping watch."

She stepped toward me then reached up to the paper towel dispenser above the sink and laid a protective layer of towels over the vanity.

"Get up on the sink and spread your legs for me," she instructed. "I need to fuck you right now. I've been dreaming about this ever since I saw you."

"That makes *two* of us," I sighed, turning around to face her while I lifted myself up onto the sink, splaying my knees against my naked breasts.

Elsa took one look at my glistening pussy and hiked up her skirt, revealing her bald pussy framed between black garter stockings.

"I *knew* you were naked under there," I smiled, feeling my juices beginning to run over my perineum all the way down to my throbbing rosebud.

"Would I have it any other way?" she said, pressing her mound against mine as she locked lips with me and pressed my back against the cold glass mirror.

"Mmm," I hummed, feeling her wetness touching mine. "Fuck me, Elsa. I've been waiting for this a long time."

Elsa lifted her knee and extended her right leg, placing her foot against the mirror beside me. Her legs were separated like a pair of open scissors, with our pussies grinding together as we moaned in each other's mouths. For a moment, my mind reeled at the audacity of what we were doing, but it didn't take long for me to begin feeling the rising tide of pleasure spreading throughout my body. Elsa had already revealed her incredible flexibility to me in our prior erotic encounters, but this new technique with her fucking me in a perfect split took me to a whole new level of sexual intensity.

"*Oh God,*" I panted as I listened to our wet labia smacking together while we ground our pussies against one another. "Are you still carrying those love balls inside you?"

"You tell *me,*" Elsa grunted as I felt her buttock muscles contract against my sweaty palms.

Suddenly, I felt the slippery balls pass out of her pussy into mine as her pussy began contracting in the initial stages of orgasm.

"Come with me, Jade," she panted. "I want to feel you spray all over me like you did in the sauna."

"*Fuck* yes," I hissed, feeling my climax suddenly overtake me from the feeling of Elsa's balls swirling around inside me. "I'm cumming, Elsa!" I groaned. "I'm cumming so hard!"

As my walls contracted tightly over the steel balls and I began squirting all over Elsa's pussy, the balls suddenly spurt back out as we grunted in unison from the feeling of the slippery orbs rubbing between our slits. We tried to remain as quiet as I could in the narrow confines of the lavatory, but it was difficult to stifle our screams of mutual ecstasy as we ground our hips together on the shaking vanity.

When the two of us came down from our powerful climaxes, I peered down, noticing that I'd soaked Elsa's black stockings with my juices.

"Sorry, sweetie," I said, shaking my head. "But I couldn't help myself. When you passed me the balls, I had the hardest climax I've had in a long time."

"Not to worry, babe," Elsa smiled, reaching into her purse beside the counter. "We flight attendants come prepared for every emergency."

As she began to pull out a new pair of stockings, we heard a tap on the door. Fearing we'd be caught by a passenger wanting to use the lavatory, my heart began thumping wildly as my eyes widened in fright. Elsa held a finger to her lips then tapped back twice on our side of the door, and the person on the other side tapped back quickly three times in succession. She smiled back at me then opened the door as Astrid squeezed in next to us.

"What the...?" I said, pinching my eyebrows in surprise. "Who'll be our lookout in case another passenger needs to use the washroom?"

"Everybody's completely passed out and sleeping peacefully," Astrid said. "We've got a few more minutes to have a little fun. I couldn't resist. Listening to you guys has gotten me all worked up."

"We were *that* obvious?" I asked.

"Only if you were standing next to the door. The sound of the jet engines drowned out most of the noise."

"Okay," Elsa said. "But we'll have to act fast. Let's let Jade take the driver's seat this time. I'll listen for any passenger pings next to the door."

Astrid hiked up her skirt and leaned back against the sink, pulling me toward her, rubbing her mound against my slippery pubis.

"Who's wearing the balls *this* time?" she smiled, peering toward Elsa.

Elsa passed Astrid the glistening balls and she slipped them inside her pussy, then she pulled me closer and began kissing me hard on the lips. Although we were standing in an upright missionary position this time, we were able to angle our hips just enough to touch our clits as we ground our pussies together. As I began to feel my pleasure rapidly escalating, thinking our little tryst couldn't possibly get any more erotic, suddenly Elsa stepped behind me and thrust her fingers into my snatch as she began finger-fucking me from behind.

"Yes, Jade!" Astrid panted, feeling Elsa rocking our hips together. "I

want to feel you cream all over me when you cum. Fuck me with your pretty American pussy."

Feeling Astrid's pussy grinding against mine with Elsa finger-fucking me from behind as she squeezed my tits was a sensory over-load. Within seconds, I began climaxing once again as I squirted a stream of powerful jets inside Astrid's hole while we moaned into each other's mouths, gripping each other tightly. Elsa pressed her own mound hard against my quivering buttocks as the three of us groaned in simultaneous ecstasy with the cabin full of passengers just outside the door seeming a million miles away.

When we all recovered from our climaxes and realized what a mess we'd made, the girls quickly changed stockings while I cleaned up the room. When we finally collected ourselves and prepared to leave, Elsa placed her ear to the door and nodded.

"I'll go first to make sure the way is clear," she said. "If everything looks good, I'll tap twice then you can both come out."

Astrid and I nodded, then Elsa opened the door and closed it quickly behind us. Within a few seconds, we heard a soft double-tap and the two of us exited the washroom as I made my way back to my seat past the still-sleeping passengers. But when I got to my chair, I peered over at the woman sitting next to me and she opened one eyelid, smiling at me.

Fuck, I thought. *We've been made.*

But seeing that she wasn't overly perturbed by the incident, I settled back into my seat, feeling the dampness of Astrid's and Elsa's juices clinging to my pussy pressing up against my moist panties. I glanced toward the front of the cabin and saw the girls sitting quietly beside one another in their jump seats with a sexy glow still on their cheeks. I smiled at them and mouthed the words *Thank You*, blowing each of them a kiss.

Seconds later, the woman sitting next to me pressed her call button and when Astrid walked down the aisle to attend to her, she asked for a blanket. When Astrid returned with the cover, the woman placed it over her lap and moments later I noticed her hand slip underneath it as she began to stroke herself between her legs. Sitting in the middle row of seats, she wasn't able to make direct eye contact with Astrid or Elsa, so she turned her head and smiled at me. As I saw her eyes begin to glaze over in self pleasure, I smiled back at her with our shared secret.

It looked like I wasn't going to be the *only* one enjoying a little mile-high thrill on our trip back from Sweden.

VOLUME FIVE

THE THERAPIST

1

———

"**E**very time I see you, I want to tell one of those bad gynecologist jokes," I said to my sex therapist friend Hannah at our weekly luncheon.

Hannah rolled her eyes as she took another bite of her salad. Her practice seemed to be the never-ending butt of jokes among our friends, but she'd learned to take the digs with good humor.

"Well you know I'm a far cry from a gynecologist, but I could use a little laugh today, so if you really need to get it out of your system, lay it on me."

"Ok, so this old lady goes to see her dentist," I started. "When her appointment is called, she sits in the chair, lowers her underpants, and raises her legs..."

"Uh huh," Hannah murmured, lifting a glass of soda water to her lips to signal her disinterest.

"So the dentist says," I continued, 'Excuse me, but I'm not a gynecologist.'"

I paused long enough for Hannah to begin swallowing her water. "'I know,' said the old lady. 'I want you to take my husband's teeth out.'"

Hannah lurched forward, spewing her soda water all over her salad as she raised her hand to her mouth, coughing loudly.

"Are you okay?" I said, glancing at the surrounding restaurant patrons alarmed by the sudden commotion at our table.

"Y–yeah," Hannah gagged. "The water just went down the wrong way. I wasn't expecting that punchline."

"Pretty good, right?" I smiled.

"Better than most, I'll grant you," she nodded. "But I don't know why you guys always make fun of my practice. *Someone* has to help all the sexually dysfunctional people out there."

"I know," I said, frowning sheepishly. "It's just hard to imagine what goes on in your office when people talk candidly about their sex lives."

"You'd be surprised," Hannah said, taking another swig of water to clear her throat. "In fact, I was thinking of inviting you to one of my sessions sometime."

I pinched my eyebrows and shook my head, surprised at her offer.

"As a *patient* or as an observer?"

"You don't need any help with your sex life," she said. "You're already miles ahead of me with all your wild escapades and adventures. I'd like to present you as more of a role model for what a healthy, sexually uninhibited person looks like."

"What would you have me *do* exactly? Don't you have to protect patient-doctor privilege? I thought you guys had to keep everything at arms-length, so to speak."

"I've been experimenting with some different strategies lately," Hannah smiled. "Let's just say I've been trying out some more *active* therapeutic techniques."

"No way!" I said, widening my eyes as I rested my cocktail on the table so as not to spill it. "Isn't that against the rules? I thought you had to maintain a certain degree of professional distance or risk losing your license."

"I still do. The only difference is now I encourage them to practice some of the prescribed self-empowerment techniques in my *office* instead of at home, so I can coach and guide them more actively. Besides, everybody signs a waiver before we take it to the next level."

"Holy shit!" I said, shaking my glass incredulously. "While you *watch* them touch themselves intimately?"

"Sometimes," Hannah nodded. "But most patients prefer to be concealed behind a protective screen when they first start the process."

"So you basically guide them through a facilitated *masturbation* session?"

"In a manner of speaking, yes. I find most patients need a little more active engagement to get them over the hump becoming comfortable enjoying sex with another person. You'd be surprised how many sexually dysfunctional women there are out there."

"So most of your patients are women?"

"Yes–I find them much more interesting to work with."

"Oh my God," I panted, beginning to feel my panties moisten under my tight jeans. "I'd love to be a fly on the wall in one of these sessions. How do you manage to stay focused when things start to heat up? Don't you get aroused while these women pleasure themselves?"

Hannah shifted uncomfortably in her chair, signaling for the waiter to bring her another cocktail.

"I do. At first, I just kind of squirmed in my chair and squeezed my legs together in frustration. But I've discovered a more animated way to keep myself stimulated while I watch my patients enjoying themselves."

My eyes flew open as the fluid in my cocktail glass began to tremble.

"You stick a *vibrator* down your pants?!" I said. "Isn't that kind of noisy? How do you hide that from your patients?"

"It's not just *any* vibrator," Hannah said with a crooked grin. "Our friend Cheryl from the local Babeland store introduced me to a new kind of toy. It's designed by a woman to mimic the touch and movement of real fingers and lips. It doesn't buzz so much as *hum* as it undulates both inside and on the outside of your vulva."

"Jesus!" I squealed, furrowing my brow in frustration. "Just when I thought I had the full collection of the latest toys. What does this thing look like?"

Hannah opened up her purse and passed me a large finger-shaped device attached to a hollow cone at the base.

"I just happen to carry one with me wherever I go," she said. "See for yourself."

I peered at the strange-looking object, stroking the soft silicone surface gently.

"It sure doesn't look like anything I've seen before. How does it work if it doesn't vibrate?"

"The long finger-shaped appendage goes inside you and bends in a series of come-hither motions against your G-spot. Give it a try by tapping the control button on the base one time."

I pressed the button and the finger began waving toward me like some kind of animatronic alien finger.

"*What the fuck*?" I said. "That's insane! It moves just like a real finger. And it hardly makes a sound."

"That the best part. You can use it anywhere. Even in a crowded restaurant. You should give it a try. Pretend that you're reclining on a couch in my office."

I glanced around the table to make sure no one else had seen the strange device that I was fondling at the table.

"It's tempting," I said, peering into the orifice at the top of the cone. "But what's with this little hole near the bottom of the device? What goes on there?"

"See for yourself," Hannah smiled. "Tap the button a second time. You might be in for a bit of a surprise."

I tapped the button again and a long, tongue-shaped object pushed up out of the hole and began undulating like a hypnotic snake against my palm.

My eyes grew wide as saucers as Hannah nodded at me with a huge smirk.

"Like I said," she grinned. "It's not a vibrator so much as a *replicator*. Doesn't it remind you of a real finger and tongue?"

"In a weird, perverted, *ET* kind of way–yeah."

Hannah lowered her gaze and nodded toward my midsection.

"You've got to feel it down there to really appreciate it. Go ahead–give it a try. No one needs to know besides us girls."

"Seriously?" I said. "Right here?!"

"Why not? There's a long skirt surrounding the table. You can loosen your pants and insert it inside you without anyone knowing. Let me have a little bit of fun watching you pleasure yourself for a change. We haven't been together that way in quite a while."

"I have to admit," I huffed. "I *am* insanely horny right now. I'm dying to try this thing out. But what are you going to do while I amuse myself?"

"I'm going to eat my salad like we're having a normal luncheon. This is all about *you* girl, don't worry about me. Knock yourself out."

"I can't believe I'm thinking about doing this," I said, watching the tongue slither back into its hole as I turned the toy off temporarily.

"It should be pretty easy to insert it if you're already properly worked up," Hannah said, lifting her glass to her lips.

I glanced to both sides of our table to make sure nobody else was watching, then reached under the tablecloth and unzipped my jeans, pulling them down to the floor. I could feel my juices already pooling on the wooden chair between my legs as I lowered the device under the table.

"Just be sure to position it so the hole is over your clit," Hannah whispered.

"I'm all over that," I nodded, slowly inserting the bulbous tip into my opening.

It slipped inside my slit smoothly, and I gasped as I pushed it all the way up inside me.

"It's not like just *any* old finger, is it?" Hannah grinned.

"No," I panted. "It's longer and fatter than most."

"It's designed with the ideal shape and form to stimulate your G-spot. If you've got it pressed all the way inside, turn it on to see what it feels like when it's animated."

I glanced around me nervously, watching the other restaurant patrons lost in conversation with their partners.

"Are you sure I'm going to be able to control myself in full view of all these customers? What if I break out into a Meg Ryan in front of all these people?"

"That'll be up to you to keep things under control as much as you can. But if not, what's the worst that can happen? Just like in the movie, everybody will want to know what you ordered that made you so happy."

"Very funny," I said, fumbling to find the control button on the base of the unit resting over my mound.

I pressed the button and began squirming in my chair as the long pointed finger began caressing me like no lover I ever had.

"Uhnn," I groaned, feeling the unusual stimulation inside my pussy.

"Not too bad, is it?" Hannah smiled. "Imagine all that going on while you're watching one of my patients pleasuring themselves."

"Is that really *possible*?" I said, getting even more turned on at the thought of watching one of her clients playing with herself in Hannah's private office.

"I've been thinking about it for a while," Hannah nodded. "It's the logical next step in the process of learning to become fully functional in a paired relationship. I've already had a few of my patients suggest they'd like me to guide them through their first encounter with another partner."

"You know how I like to *watch*," I groaned, as my eyes began to glaze over from the delicate sensation of the long finger rubbing up against my G-spot.

Hannah crossed her legs under the table and began to bob up and down as she flexed her buttocks and thighs together watching me get off.

"I do," she said, lifting her cocktail glass off the table and sliding her tongue around the rim suggestively. "Try the tongue action now."

"You're such a tease," I hissed, reaching under the tablecloth and tapping the control button one more time.

When I felt the flexible appendage push out of the hole and begin rolling over my hard clit, I bent over my place setting, grasping the handles of my chair tightly.

"That's it, babe," Hannah purred. "Feel the rhythm. Close your eyes and imagine it's your fantasy partner licking your pussy. Surrender to the feeling..."

"Is this how you do it with your clients?" I panted. "Talking to them all sexy while they play with themselves?"

"Sometimes," Hannah smiled. "Or sometimes I just let them do most of the vocalization while they tell me what they're doing behind the screen."

I spread my knees further apart imagining myself in one of her sessions.

"Do they ever get to the point where they're comfortable letting you watch them?"

"That's the ultimate goal. I've had a number of clients reach that level already. But I'd like to try taking it one step further. That's where you come in–"

"Tell me, Han," I moaned, beginning to lose myself in the fantasy. "Tell me what you want me to do with your sexy patients."

"We'll start out slowly at first," she instructed. "We'll just have you listen to them moan and purr as they begin the process of self-discovery behind the safety of their protective screen. But you'll have to be quiet at first to not distract their self-focus."

"At *this* point," I said, beginning to feel the pleasure spreading over my entire body. "That might be enough. With this amazing device doing its thing, I could probably get off listening to the sound of running water."

"That's the intent," Hannah laughed. "At least for my clients. But in order for them to become truly uninhibited and be able to function competently, the next step would be for the two of you to emerge from your hiding places and become comfortable watching each other in a face-to-face setting."

"*Fuck, yes,*" I panted. "If I can help another soul learn to enjoy the full pleasures of lesbian sex, count me in!"

"I know *you* won't have any trouble participating in this next phase of the process," Hannah smiled. "Just try to keep some of your more extreme methods in check for a while so you don't scare away my customers."

"I promise to keep my big dildos at home if you insist," I smirked.

"Once we get them feeling comfortable touching themselves and achieving climax in this voyeur scenario, the last step will be for the two of you to join together on the same couch and explore each other with more direct contact."

"Can I break out some of my favorite moves then?"

"If you find your partner is responding appropriately. Just be careful to always be gentle and focused on her needs. If you get to the point where she feels comfortable getting more inventive, by all means–"

"Oh, I've got the *means* alright," I moaned, imaging myself straddling one of her patients with her legs splayed wide apart as we ground our pussies together and I watched her come all over me. "How soon can we set this up?"

"I've got a certain patient in mind. She's young and never been with another woman before. She's had some unfulfilling experiences with men and confided that she's always fantasized about being with a woman. We'll just have to ease her into it carefully. Are you up for the opportunity, assuming she's game?"

"You know I am," I grunted, pressing harder down against the artificial tongue. "But first, tell me more about this girl…"

"She's nineteen, a sophomore in college, with a cheerleader's body–"

"She's athletic then?"

"Oh yes," Hannah smiled. "Tight ass, firm tits, and legs that could wrap all the way around you while you tribbed her virgin pussy–"

"Oh God, Han," I moaned. "I can't take it any longer. Sign me up– I want to taste her sweet pussy in my mouth…"

"Yes, Jade," Hannah purred. "Let it go, hun. Surrender to the feeling–"

As I imagined the co-ed writhing in ecstasy sitting on my face, the pleasure generated by the lifelike sex toy suddenly peaked, and I bit my lip as I began convulsing in my chair. I'd never fought so hard to remain quiet during a powerful orgasm in my entire life. There was something about the experience of cumming surrounded by scores of oblivious restaurant patrons that made the experience all the more erotic. While I twisted and squirmed in my chair, Hannah smiled as she raised her glass in toast to me.

"Congratulations, Jade," she said. "You've just passed the first test with flying colors."

2

———————

With every passing day after our luncheon, I grew increasingly excited about the idea of participating in one of Hannah's guided therapy sessions. When she finally called me back, I almost dropped my phone fumbling to answer it.

"Han?" I answered the phone expectantly.

"Are you sure you're up for this?" Hannah asked.

"Are you kidding me?" I said. "It's all I've been thinking about since I last saw you."

"I've got another session scheduled with my target client for this Thursday at eleven a.m. Are you available?"

"With the young co-ed?"

"Yes."

"Absolutely!" I gushed.

"Ok," Hannah said. "We're going to have to set this up carefully. I don't want to put too much pressure on either one of you during this initial encounter. I think it's better if she doesn't even know you're there at first. I'll talk to her while she begins to explore her body behind the safety of the protective screen, then broach the subject of introducing a potential partner at the next session."

"Okay," I said. "But where will you hide me?"

"As strange as it may sound, I think the only safe place to be sure you're not discovered is in my closet. You can open the door a crack and listen if you promise to be absolutely quiet the entire time. That way, I can protect her identity in the event she doesn't wish to escalate things to the next level."

I shook my head at the idea of spying on her like a peeping Tom, but the dampness in my panties betrayed my true feelings.

"I'll feel like a bit of a lech hiding in the closet, but if that's what it'll take to make sure she's comfortable, I can work with that."

"Okay then," Hannah said. "Meet me at my office at 10:45 and I'll get you situated. And remember–not even a peep."

"I promise to be on my best behavior," I smiled. "If I can stay silent surrounded by a hundred restaurant customers, I think I can handle one uptight schoolgirl."

"And don't bring any toys either. I don't want to take the chance she'll hear anything other than my soothing voice."

"Not even your special vibrator that doesn't make any noise?"

"I'm not sure I can trust you with that thing. Besides, it's already going to be put to good use while you're in the closet."

"No fair!" I protested. "*You'll* be the one having all the fun!"

"I'm sure you can find other ways to amuse yourself," Hannah said. "You'll have plenty of chances to get more actively engaged during the next session. Just don't trip over anything in there when things start to heat up."

As soon as Hannah hung up, I rushed into my bedroom and positioned my dressing room mirror in front of my clothes closet. Then I opened the door a crack and imagined it was the schoolgirl I was watching while I jilled myself to a quick orgasm.

This should be interesting, I thought, quivering in the darkness. *I just hope her patient will find it as erotic as I do, knowing someone else is on the other side of the curtain.*

On the day of the scheduled session, I arrived fifteen minutes early as requested, while Hannah reiterated the ground rules and gave me final instructions. She made me promise that I wouldn't open the door until her client was safely behind the protective screen. She knew she was already pushing the boundary of professional ethics, and she wanted to make sure that her patient's identity would be protected until the girl felt comfortable introducing another person into the mix.

When I got into the closet, I pushed the coats to one side to produce an open space for me, then I peered through the louvers as I heard a soft tap on Hannah's office door. The slats were angled downward, so I could only see the floor a few feet ahead of me, but that was enough to get my heart racing in excitement already.

"Good morning, Haley," I heard Hannah say as two shadows crossed the floor in front of me. "Can I get you a coffee or tea? It's a bit chilly out there today, and you probably need to warm up."

"I'm fine, thank you," a young woman's voice spoke softly. "I'm pretty nervous about today's session and I don't think I should be holding any hot beverages in my trembling hands."

"There's no need to worry," Hannah assured the girl. "We're going to take things slowly, at your own pace. May I take your coat?"

"Yes, thank you," the girl said.

I heard the rustling of clothes then the sound of footfalls moving toward the closet. The door on the opposite side of the closet opened and Hannah reached in to fetch an open hanger, then she hung the girl's coat over the crossbar. I could smell her perfume on the garment, and my pussy twitched when I realized how close she was to me on the other side of the door. But neither Hannah nor I so much as made eye contact, to protect the secrecy of our little ruse.

"Have a seat, please," Hannah said, and I heard the sound of the girl reclining on the office divan.

"If you remember from our last session," Hannah continued, "we talked about trying something a little different today. You shared your discomfort about touching yourself intimately based on your prior family history, and that you thought it might be helpful to have me coach you through a private session. Are you still feeling comfortable taking it to this next level?"

"I think so," Haley said. "But you mentioned the possibility of my having a bit more privacy. I'm not sure I'm ready to have you watch me just yet."

"Of course," Hannah said. "It'll be easier for you to concentrate on exploring your body and focus on what you're feeling without any outside distractions. I can move the linen screen between the two of us to protect your privacy, but I'd also like to place this long dressing mirror in front of your couch so you can watch yourself and begin to get more comfortable with your body. Will that work for you?"

"I suppose so," Haley said, hesitating. "Do you have any expectations for today's session? I mean, in terms of achieving climax or anything like that?"

"None whatsoever," Hannah said. "This is all about you becoming comfortable in your own skin and beginning the process of self-exploration. The only desire I have is that you learn to relax and accept the beauty of your own body. This is a journey, not a destination. You need to learn how to love *yourself* before you can begin to think about loving someone else."

Oh, she's good, I thought. If only every girl could have this kind of advice when they're first experiencing the strange feelings of puberty and early adulthood. Far too many parents make their kids think sex is dirty and that enjoying any kind of carnal pleasure before marriage is sinful. For a moment, I reflected back on my own awkward attempts at sex with my first husband, realizing how much time and pleasure I'd forsaken until I learned to explore my sexuality on my own and with other like-minded women.

I listened to the sound of furniture moving across the floor as Hannah positioned the mirror in front of Haley's settee then placed the curtain between their two chairs.

"Does that make you feel more comfortable?" Hannah asked the girl.

"Yes, thank you," Haley said.

"Good. Now first, I just want you to look at yourself fully clothed in the mirror. Look at your pretty face and the curves of your figure and recognize that you're a beautiful woman who was designed to enjoy the natural pleasures of your body. And that this is also part of the natural process of pairing with a partner and enjoying the shared union that is part of the human experience."

"Okay..." Haley said with a hesitating lilt.

As I listened to her soft voice, my mind raced imagining what she looked like lying on the divan, watching herself in the mirror.

"But first you need to get fully comfortable in your own skin," Hannah said. "And begin to experience the pleasures that you've been naturally endowed with as a healthy young woman. Unfortunately, our society has learned to cover up our bodies as if they're a shameful thing we should hide. I want you to see your body as a beautiful thing and recognize the pleasures it can deliver to you, both when you're alone and with a partner."

Damn straight, I thought, feeling the blood rushing to my pussy as I reflected back on my own first tentative explorations of my young body that led to my first climax.

"Now I want you to take off your blouse and your bra,'"Hannah continued. "And lie back against the chair as you examine your body and begin to explore some of your erogenous areas."

I heard the sound of soft rustling behind the screen, followed by awkward silence.

"Can you see your naked torso in the mirror in front of you?" Hannah asked.

"Yes..." Haley said softly.

"Look at your breasts and examine their shape. Did you know that every woman has her own unique shape? Some have large breasts, some have small breasts, some have pointy breasts, and some have floppy breasts. It's all part of the female expression and what makes you unique."

More awkward silence.

"Do you like the shape of your breasts, Haley?" Hannah said.

"I suppose so…"

"I want you to cup them in your hands and feel how soft and pleasant they feel to be held and coddled. A woman's breasts are a beautiful thing, and they serve many purposes. Besides feeding a newborn child, their shape is meant to attract other partners whose bodies you can likewise enjoy and appreciate. And of course, your breasts can be a source of intense internal pleasure for yourself. Did you know that some women can climax just from the feeling of their babies suckling on their teats?"

"I had no idea," Haley said.

While Hannah talked the girl through the process of self-examination, I mimicked her movements and gestures, trying to imagine how she felt and how her body was responding. I unbuttoned my blouse and opened my bra, feeling an electric charge race through my body as I felt the fullness of my breasts in my hands.

"Now I want you to pinch your nipples gently between your thumbs and forefingers as you cup your breasts and roll them between your fingers, telling me what you feel."

"It tingles a little bit," Haley confessed.

"In a good way?"

"Yes–I think so."

"Do you notice any changes to the size and shape of your nipples?"

"Yes," Haley said. "They're growing larger and firmer."

"That's another one of the amazing reactions our bodies experience when our erogenous zones are properly stimulated. Do you like the feeling when you touch your breasts in this way, Haley?"

"Yes," she panted softly.

The girl's visceral reaction to touching herself sent a chill down my spine as I felt myself getting wetter and wetter by the moment.

"Look at your body in the mirror as you touch yourself. Do you see your chest flushing and your breasts subtly changing shape?"

"Yes."

"That's from your blood rushing to the area to provide more oxygen and nutrients to feed the increased stimulation. Isn't it wonderful how our bodies naturally respond when we stimulate it in a pleasant way?"

"Mmm," Haley purred.

"Now I want you to bend your head down and lift one of your breasts toward your mouth. You've been blessed with larger breasts than most, and if you can suck and lick your nipples, I want you to tell me how it feels."

Soon after, I heard the sound of liquid sloshing and the smacking of lips. I knew that Haley was sucking her plump nipples, and the thought of it sent rivers of fluid running down the inside of my legs. I was glad that I'd chosen to wear a dress instead of jeans so I'd have freer access to my pussy in the tight confines of Hannah's closet.

"How does that feel?" Hannah asked.

"Heavenly," Haley sighed. "I've never really explored my body in this way before."

"You'll be amazed at all the ways you and your partner can create exciting sensations like these using different techniques and body parts to explore the different areas of your body. Look up at your nipples in the mirror every now and then, but don't let me stop you from continuing your exploration."

I could hear the sloshing and smacking sounds increasing in frequency and pitch, along with Haley's moans and sighs. I had to bite my lip to keep from moaning myself, as I imagined what she must have been feeling at this moment.

"What do you see and feel?" Hannah asked.

"The dark ring around my nipples is getting smaller and my nipples are getting harder the more I lick and suck them."

"Mmm, that's good," Hannah said.

I could tell Hannah was getting just as turned on as I was from the exchange, and I wondered if she'd turned on her vibrator yet.

"Mix up the way you stimulate your nipples," she said. "Try circling your tongue around the perimeter and flicking it over the ends of your nipples every now and then. Most of the pleasure in exploring our bodies is discovered from the many different ways we can stimulate ourselves and others. Squeeze your breasts with your hands, pinch your nipples, suck and play with them as you lose yourself in the moment."

"It feels good," Haley panted. "I think I'm ready to try some of those other new techniques you mentioned now."

I smiled when I realized Haley was losing herself in the process and beginning to surrender to the pleasurable feelings flooding her body.

"Let's get comfortable seeing your *entire* body in the nude then," Hannah continued. "I want you to take off the rest of your clothes and throw them to the side. There are so many other ways to give yourself pleasure."

I heard some more rustling of clothes, this time more urgent-sounding, and the telltale sound of clothes dropping to the floor. It was obvious to me that Haley was getting more and more worked up and that she no longer cared if her clothes got a little wrinkled or dirty.

After the rustling sound stopped, Hannah paused for a moment to let the silence in the room escalate the sexual tension. Her professional technique was working for more than just her client, as I froze with my hand still as a statue against my dripping pussy while I imagined the pretty schoolgirl looking at her naked body on the chaise lounge chair.

"Are you fully naked now, Haley?" Hannah asked.

"Yes," the girl said.

"Examine the curve of your profile for a moment. See the way your waist tapers and the swelling of your hips above your long, shapely legs. Do you think you're beautiful, Haley?"

"Yes," she said. "I feel good all over."

"Good," Hannah said. "Now I want you to spread your legs and knees apart a little bit so you can examine your private area. Can you see your skin glistening on your vulva and on the inside of your thighs?"

"Yes," Haley panted.

"That means your body is enjoying the stimulation you've provided so far and that you're feeling aroused viewing your own body. Can you see the slit between your legs?"

"Yes–"

"I want you to run your hands gently down the front of your torso, feeling the softness of the skin on your abdomen..."

"My tummy is trembling," Haley said.

"That's a natural reaction to the excitement you feel as you caress yourself and move closer to your magical place."

"Magical place?"

"You'll see what I mean soon enough. Can you see the natural hairs covering your private area?"

"Yes," Haley said.

Both Hannah and I guessed that a girl this young and innocent wouldn't have learned yet to trim her pubic hair in the manner of the modern custom.

"I want you to run your fingers through your bush and tell me what you feel."

For a moment I envied the virgin schoolgirl with her natural muff. It had been a long time since I'd felt the wonderful feeling of my pubic hairs being caressed and stroked in this way. By way of consolation, I raised my slippery fingers up from my crotch and spread my juices over my bare mound.

"It feels kind of ticklish," Haley said from behind the screen. "But in a good way. I feel all warm and tingly inside."

"That's your body's way of saying it's enjoying the sensation of being touched this way. Now the blood is rushing to an entirely different area of your body. Can you feel yourself becoming wetter and wetter around your opening?"

"Yes," Haley said. "It's a good thing you put a blanket down over your chair. Otherwise, I'd be making a mess of your pretty office."

"That's perfect," Hannah said. "I'd like nothing more than for you to make a mess of my office. That just means that you're enjoying the experience and that your body is reacting the way it was meant to."

"I can feel things beginning to heat up down there," Haley grunted. "And there's other changes too–"

"Spread your legs further apart now and tell me what changes you see. And what you *feel*."

"I can see my lips are getting wetter and darker. And my little bean is getting plumper and harder. I feel like I'm tingling all over now..."

"Move your hands between your thighs and feel the slippery wetness as you caress the sides of your labia. How does that feel?"

"It feels *good*," Haley panted. "It's so warm and wet. I'm feeling some other sensations now..."

"Isn't it wonderful how good you can make yourself feel just by gently exploring your body and appreciating your natural beauty?"

"Yes, Dr. Marshall."

"Please, call me Hannah. At this point, we don't need to stay so informal, plus it will make it easier for you to vocalize what you're feeling. Now, I want you to explore a very special place on your body. Trace your fingers up along the edges of your labia until they meet at the top, then touch your little nub and tell me what you feel."

"*Huh!*" Haley gasped. "Oh, that feels–different. It's a much more intense type of tingling now."

By now I was rubbing my button furiously as I imagined Haley playing with her clit for the first time. As I peered through the slats trying desperately to catch any sight of her shadow or movement on the reflective floor, I could hear the soft sound of my own juices as I became more and more excited by the sensory deprivation of being locked in the closet.

"Yes," Hannah said, encouraging Haley on. "We women are lucky to be endowed with the most sensitive organ on the human body. Our clitorises are bestowed with more than eight thousand nerve endings–more per square inch than even on the end of a man's penis. Rub your fingers softly over your jewel and close your eyes as you savor the feeling."

"Oh God," Haley moaned. "That feels so good. I had no idea I could make myself feel this way."

"We're just getting started exploring all the possibilities," Hannah said, her own voice starting to become ragged. "Run your fingers over your clit, trying different movements. Sometimes it's nice to pinch it gently between your fingers, and sometimes it feels good to rub your fingers in circles over your button. Can you see anything *else* changing in your vulva as you rub yourself this way?"

"Yes," Haley groaned. "My lips are getting puffier, and they're beginning to separate a bit."

"*Fuck me*," I groaned under my breath, wishing I could be looking into the same mirror that Haley was viewing at this precise moment. *How I'd love to fuck her sweet little pussy right now.*

"That's perfectly normal and healthy," Hannah purred. "That's just your body's way of saying that it's ready to accept another partner into the equation. Do you think you'd like to try that someday soon?"

"Maybe," Haley said. "But right now I'm having too much fun all by myself. I'm beginning to feel some different feelings now. The tingling is getting much more intense. It almost feels like I have to pee or something..."

"That means you're getting closer to reaching the apex of your pleasure," Hannah said, shifting in her chair. "Close your eyes now and focus on your body as you surrender to the pleasure. Don't worry if things start to get pretty intense. Just lose yourself in the process..."

"Yes, doc–I mean Hannah," Haley squeaked. "I feel it now. It feels like a wave is falling over me. A big, beautiful wall of pleasure engulfing me..."

"Yes, Haley," Hannah mewed. "Let it consume you. Surrender to the passion inside your body."

"Oh God! Oh God!" Haley whimpered. "It feels so good. Something is happening. I feel it coming over me–. Uhnnn! Uhnnn! Uhnnn!"

As I listened to Haley having her first powerful orgasm, I lost all control and began squirting over the floor of Hannah's closet as my pussy clamped together in multiple contractions while I leaned against the wall to steady myself. I'd never heard anything so erotic in my entire life, and my whole body was trembling at the thought of meeting her face-to-face at our next session.

When Haley finally stopped moaning and silence filled the room, I could hear Hannah shifting again in her chair. I wondered if she'd been unable to control herself and had had a powerful orgasm of her own listening to Haley. With that lifelike sex toy embedded in her pussy, I couldn't imagine how she'd able to hold back.

"How does it feel to experience the natural pleasures of being a woman, Haley?" she said.

"Oh my God," Haley panted. "I had no idea I had this inside of me. I want more–"

"There's so much more for you to experience, young lady. I encourage you to experiment with more self-exploration before our next session. Of course, the ultimate pleasure of being a woman happens when you get to *share* this pleasure with another partner. Do you think you might be ready to try this at our next meeting?"

"Um–maybe. But how will that work? I don't think I'm quite ready to jump right into an intimate relationship with a complete stranger."

"With your permission," Hannah said, "I'd like to invite another patient to the session who's expressed similar feelings about being with another woman. We can start slowly at first with the two of you just watching and talking to one another before we consider taking it to the next stage. You should always feel completely comfortable with your partner before agreeing to share this kind of intimacy."

"That does sound interesting," Haley said. "Would we be separated by protective screens again?"

"Only if you both want it that way. But something tells me you're ready to discover for yourself how much higher it can elevate the experience watching another woman pleasuring herself with you at the same time."

"Yes," Haley said. "I think I might like that."

"Let me know before your next session if you'd like to meet this new girl. Because she's definitely ready to meet you."

No shit, I muttered under my breath as my pussy continued spasming over my fingers firmly embedded inside my hole.

I had no idea know how I'd be able to keep it together for a whole week before I met this girl again. I smiled as my juices streamed down the insides of my thighs.

I'll just have to practice as much as I can in the meantime to get ready.

3

———

The intervening week before Haley's next scheduled session felt like the longest week of my life. I couldn't stop thinking about what she looked like and how she'd react to watching me respond to Hannah's instruction the way she had. I spent long hours lying on my couch with my dressing mirror propped up in front of me, fantasizing that it was Haley watching me instead of myself.

I must have cum a hundred times contorting myself into different positions trying to make myself look as sexy and alluring as possible. I didn't want to take any chance that she wouldn't respond positively to me in this shared therapy session. Beyond my desire for her to enjoy the experience to the fullest extent possible, I didn't want anything getting in the way of her moving on to the final step in her journey of sexual awakening. Every time I thought about actually touching her, my pussy throbbed and I had to tear my clothes off once again to quell the yearning desire within me.

When the appointment day finally arrived, I spent most of the morning trying on different outfits I thought might strike the right balance between sexually enticing and emotionally guarded. After all, Hannah was presenting me as another repressed patient who'd reached out for help overcoming her fear of intimacy with other women. I finally decided on a pleated mid-length skirt with inch-high pumps and a creamy silk blouse that hugged my breasts just enough to highlight the fullness of my bosom.

Hannah had asked me to arrive at her office five minutes after the hour so she could prep Haley first and confirm that she still wished to proceed as intended. The plan was for her to send me a quick text with either a smiling or frowning emoji to signal her readiness. When I still hadn't heard anything by 11:15, I shifted uncomfortably in her waiting room, wondering if Haley had gotten cold feet.

I couldn't blame her if she had. This whole idea was highly irregular and must have been kind of frightening for her. It was a far cry from meeting someone the natural way, getting to know them over a period of time before deciding to initiate intimate relations. But if she was too afraid to approach another woman the traditional way, I had every intention of making this experience as comfortable and uplifting as possible.

When my phone pinged and I saw the smiley-face symbol in my message thread, I stood up and nervously smoothed out the wrinkles in my blouse. I chuckled at the realization that I was just as anxious as the young schoolgirl at the prospect of our chaperoned playdate. Hannah stuck her head out her office door motioning me inside, and I straightened myself out and walked confidently into her office.

The girl was standing a few feet to Hannah's side, smiling nervously at me when our eyes met. I was surprised how young she looked in her skinny jeans, tight t-shirt, and Keds sneakers. She had long blonde hair, big bright eyes, and the plump skin of an adolescent who hadn't lost any of her youthful collagen. I must have looked ancient almost fifteen years older than her, as I pulled my shoulders back trying to lift my chest and press my breasts against my tight blouse.

Hannah turned toward the girl, arcing her arm toward me.

"Haley," she said. "This is Jade. In spite of your difference in age, I think you'll find you actually have a lot in common. I've brought the two of you together today to share some of your mutual experiences and learn to become more comfortable expressing your intimacy in the presence of another woman."

Hannah peered at the two of us and smiled.

"Would you like a drink before we get started?"

"Have you got some *tequila* behind your bar?" I joked.

"That might not be such a bad idea to help you both loosen up," Hannah chuckled. "But unfortunately, all I have to offer is coffee or tea."

"I'll have a coffee with a bit of cream and sugar then," I said.

"Tea is fine," Haley nodded.

"Cream and sugar also?" Hannah asked.

"Yes, thank you."

As Hannah turned to prepare our drinks, I moved closer toward Haley and extended my hand. She looked even prettier up close, with thick natural eyebrows and long dark lashes.

"Pleased to meet you, Haley," I said. "Hannah's told me so much about you. You're even more beautiful than she described."

Haley reached out and clasped my hand softly, and I could feel the nervous dampness in her palm as we touched for the first time.

"Thank you," she said. "You're very pretty also."

Her eyes blinked as she stole a glance down my body, peering at the cleavage formed by my push-up bra peeking out of my loosely unbuttoned blouse. My breasts were at least full size larger than hers, and I stood three or four inches taller in my elevated pumps.

"You remind me a little of Marilyn Monroe in that white blouse and skirt," she said.

"That's very kind," I smiled. "I could never hold a candle to her, though I feel a certain affinity given my own little seven-year-itch. It took me at least that long to break free of the oppressive bonds of my first marriage."

"Have you married again?"

"No–I guess I'm still discovering myself. I've kind of been looking for a change of pace lately. I never felt fully satisfied in my relationships with men."

"I've never felt comfortable approaching *either* gender, actually. My parents were pretty strict about the whole dating thing when I was growing up–"

Hannah returned from her kitchen and handed each of us a steaming mug.

"I see you two are beginning to get more comfortable," she said. "I'm glad to see you hitting it off so quickly. Would you like to get more comfortable?"

Haley and I turned to see two long chaise lounge chairs facing one another about ten feet apart, angled slightly toward Hannah's armchair positioned at the apex of the triangle. I smiled when I realized she'd done this intentionally to facilitate her own enhanced viewing of the two of us once we got loosened up.

We walked toward the settees and I paused, motioning for Haley to take the one on the left side. Both chairs were covered in a long throw blanket, and I kicked off my shoes before sitting back against the curved backrest, crossing my ankles on the end nearest Haley. It felt awkward holding my coffee in this semi-reclined position, and when I leaned over to rest it on the floor beside me, Haley did the same.

"How are you both feeling today?" Hannah said as she sat in her chair in front of us, crossing her legs sexily with her pointed pumps bouncing gently in our direction.

I had little doubt she was wearing her special sex toy under her prim business suit, and I envied her for a moment, knowing she'd have a leg up on the two of us for the rest of the session.

"Good," Haley said, with a gentle lilt.

"Better *now*," I said, smiling toward Haley.

"You've both expressed interest in exploring a same-sex relationship, but also about your reservations initiating the process given your previous experiences."

I nodded, realizing there was more than a hint of truth in her statement, even though I'd long since resolved my reticence about being with other women.

"The purpose of this session is to give you both an opportunity to become more comfortable in the presence of another woman, and to the extent you feel ready, to begin to explore the boundaries of your sexuality in the safe confines of my office. Is this still something you both feel comfortable proceeding with?"

I looked at Haley and she peered back at me, as we both nodded gently.

"Okay," Hannah said. "At first, I'd just like the two of you to gaze into each other's eyes for a moment and pause as you take a moment to acknowledge each other as willing partners and make a silent connection..."

I smiled at Haley and saw a soft flush spread over her cheeks as her pupils began to widen while she peered back at me. Even though neither of us said a thing, the longer I looked at her the more excited I got as my chest began rising and falling from my elevated respiration rate.

"Now, I want each of you to take a minute to look over each other's bodies without making any judgements or feeling self-conscious that you're checking each other out. Take a moment to appreciate the different shapes of your respective figures, and listen to how your body is reacting as you soak each other up."

I was happy to be given free license to leer at Haley's youthful figure, and as my eyes drifted down her body, I could feel my panties begin to moisten in excitement seeing the girl of my dreams reclining directly in front of me. Her breasts looked like they were painted on her body, sitting high and firm under her tight t-shirt. She had a narrow waist and slim but shapely hips, tapering to slender hourglass-shaped legs, looking all the more toned resting gently on the firm surface of her settee.

She in turn ran her gaze all over my body, pausing to stare at my full breasts pushing up against the flimsy silk fabric of my blouse. For a moment, I wished I'd decided to go braless, so she could see how she was turning me on as my nipples pressed against the soft fabric of my lace bra. After a few seconds of lingering, her eyes traced a line further down my body, pausing at the bottom of my skirt's hemline, as if hoping to catch a glimpse into the shadow between my closed legs. When her gaze reached the bottom of my feet, I wiggled my toes playfully, and she did the same with her cute sneakers. Even though we hadn't said a thing to each other for several minutes, I felt like we were already beginning to bond over our strange circumstances.

"Take a moment to revel in the beauty and diversity of the female form," Hannah whispered. "Recognize that everyone is built differently, and that these differences contribute to making each of us all the more interesting and alluring. Can you see the natural beauty within each of your own bodies and in those of your partner?"

"Yes," Haley nodded, tracing her gaze once again up to my pointed breasts.

"Absolutely," I enthused.

"Let's take this to the next level then," Hannah said. "If you feel comfortable, I'd like each of you to remove your tops and lie back in your chair while you admire one another in your undergarments."

As I slowly began unbuttoning my blouse, Haley leaned forward, pulling her t-shirt over her shoulders. When she lifted it over her head, her blonde locks fell down over the front of her cream-colored sports bra. I was a little disappointed to see her covered up so tightly, but her bra only seemed to accentuate the firmness of her perky tits.

When I unfastened the last button on my blouse, I pulled my arms out one side at a time then leaned back against the soft backrest. It felt electrifying to rest there in my lacy bra as Haley ran her eyes lustily over my exposed chest and abdomen. My brassiere was low-cut enough that she could see the tops of my dark areolas, and they puckered slightly as my hard nipples began to lift the fabric away from my skin.

"Now look at each other's bodies more closely," Hannah intoned. "Examine the shape of each other's breasts, the curvature of your waists, and the smoothness of your stomachs. What do you see that appeals to your feminine senses?"

"I like the fullness of Jade's breasts," Haley purred. "And the way the top edge of her bra angles sexily down toward her cleavage."

"Yes," Hannah said, stretching the S out the end of the word. "Being a sensual woman means we can dress up in different ways to tease and excite our partners as a precursor to more intimate relations. What do you see in Haley's body that you find most attractive, Jade?"

I paused for a moment, examining her tight belly and the subtle striations in her stomach.

"I like the line running down the middle of her abdomen from the bottom of her bra to her belly button. I wish I could be that lean and sexy once again."

"That's the beauty we share as women of different generations. Some women are more lean and chiseled, while others are more full-bodied and curvy. It's all part of the magnificent palette of the human form and what makes it so interesting for each of us to experience. Are you beginning to imagine what lies further underneath?"

"Yes..." Haley said, her cheeks flushing a crimson red.

"Oh, very definitely yes," I sighed, wishing I could jump out of my seat and tear Haley's sports bra off with my own hands.

"If you're ready then, you may remove your brassieres and begin to get more comfortable being naked in the presence of one another."

Haley hesitated for a moment, looking at me to make the first move. Fortunately, the bra I'd chosen to wear had the closure at the front, and as I pressed my fingers together unhinging the clasp and spreading the cups apart to reveal my naked breasts, I heard Haley gasp a few feet away. Her reaction only excited me more as I peered down at my tits, seeing that my nipples had already hardened and extended to their full extent. I pulled my bra off my back and threw it on the floor, and my whole body started buzzing as Haley stared at my torso with wide eyes.

Within a few seconds, she felt emboldened enough to remove her own sports bra as she pinched her thumbs under the lower band and pulled it over her head in one swift movement. Her breasts jiggled softly on her chest and I marveled at how perfectly round and symmetrical they were. They looked bigger than I imagined when I saw her fully clothed, and I began to salivate as I leered at her creamy skin and her light-colored areolas. They'd already begun to bunch up in excitement, protruding like two erasers on the end of a pencil.

Hannah paused just long moment to give each of us a chance to soak up each other's bodies. I could see Haley's eyes darting excitedly between my points as a light dew formed at the top of her chest between her breasts. This just accentuated the youthful look of her glistening skin, glowing like a sexy goddess. As my mouth watered at the thought of taking her moist nipples into my mouth, another part of me began to grow rapidly wetter.

"What are you feeling as you look each other's naked bodies?" Hannah said, interrupting our thoughts.

"I'm thinking how much I want to touch Haley right now," I confessed.

"There'll be plenty of time for that soon enough," Hannah said, admonishing me gently. "What are you feeling at this moment, Haley?"

"I'm just..." Haley panted, her moist lips parting slightly. "I'm just amazed at how gorgeous Jade's tits–I mean *breasts* are. She's looks like a supermodel to me."

"It's okay to use informal terms to describe each other's bodies," Hannah nodded. "It helps to desensitize the experience and lose yourself more readily in the feelings of arousal that you're experiencing. Are you beginning to recognize how each of you are responding to the sight of watching one another in this manner?"

"Yes," Haley said as she locked her eyes on my tingling teats.

"You have *no* idea," I smiled, peering at Haley's quivering tummy.

"I'm happy you're both responding so positively. That means you're attracted to one another and that you're becoming more comfortable with the idea of exploring a different kind of union. Are you ready to take it to the next level?"

"I think so..." Haley hesitated.

"*God* yes," I panted, feeling the wetness in my panties beginning to run down the crack of my ass.

"Why don't you both take off your lower garments now, but keep your panties on for the moment? Part of the attraction with foreplay is taking our time to build the desire and teasing our partners by withholding those things we most crave. Take a moment to look at your naked bodies, but not completely undressed yet."

I leaned forward and unclasped the latch at the back of my skirt, then lowered the zipper and pulled my skirt down the front of my legs, throwing it playfully on the floor. Haley locked eyes on me as she unfastened the front of her jeans, wiggling sexily on her divan while she pulled her pants down, then flipping off her sneakers and throwing everything on the floor beside her.

She was wearing plain white low-cut panties that stretched at least four inches below her navel. I could see the dark outline of her bush under the thin fabric, and my pussy twitched knowing I'd soon get to see her completely naked. She leaned back and fixed her gaze on my crotch while I teasingly separated my feet a few inches. I was wearing matching lace panties and the light color must have shown the giant wet spot that had formed in the fabric. But I couldn't yet see any sign of wetness in Haley's underwear, since she still had her legs closed in a protective posture.

"How does it feel to view another woman like this, nearly naked?" Hannah asked. "Are you noticing any new reactions in your body as you watch your partner disrobe?"

"Yes," Haley panted. "I'm beginning to feel that same tingling sensation I experienced at our last session. It feels like my whole body is on fire..."

"How about you, Jade?" Hannah said, smiling at me. "How do you feel sitting in front of Haley almost naked?"

"Very sexy," I said. "I'm feeling things I haven't felt in a long time."

"So it would appear," she said, glancing at the wet spot between my legs. "Now I want each of you to spread your legs a little further apart to witness the effect you're having on one another. Take a moment to recognize the reaction each of you are experiencing as you become more and more aroused looking at one another's bodies."

As I spread my legs further apart, Haley pulled her feet up a few inches, then angled her knees down onto the divan to reveal the white swath of fabric running between her legs. I could see the indentation of her slit in the tight cotton and the telltale darkness of a small wet spot in the middle of her panties. Seeing her reveal this little slice of her private anatomy raised my excitement level even higher as the wet spot in my own panties slowly spread all the way from one side to the other.

While Haley stared at the widening dark spot between my legs, I noticed her chest begin to rise and fall as she started breathing more heavily. It took every ounce of my willpower to stay seated in my settee and not sprint over to her side and take her for myself. Hannah was right about one thing. All this slow buildup was driving me more crazy with desire and just increasing my longing to touch her.

"Can you see how each of you are responding to one another the more you reveal of yourselves?" Hannah said. "Are you beginning to become more comfortable with the idea of watching another woman being intimate and moving closer to a more formal connection?"

"Yes," Haley sighed.

"*Fuck*, yes," I gushed.

"Let's remove our remaining entrapments then and revel in the naked glory of the female body. You may both remove your last vestiges of clothing if you feel comfortable. Take a moment to soak up one another's bodies and connect with your feelings. A healthy sexual relationship starts with feeling comfortable in both your and your partner's nakedness."

I raised my hips, practically tearing my panties off as I pulled them down my legs and tossing them on the floor. While I kept my legs slightly parted, Haley wriggled out of her little white panties and dropped them sexily on the floor beside her. This time, she parted her legs the same distance as mine as we both stared at each other's wet slits shining in the bright overhead lights of Hannah's office. Haley's light pubic patch formed a perfect triangle over her mound and I clenched the fabric on the divan beside me trying to keep my hands from straying any further.

"There now," Hannah purred. "That wasn't so bad, was it?"

"No," Haley said. "It was actually easier than I imagined."

"How about you, Jade? How do you feel seeing your partner fully naked in front of you?"

"I'd hardly call it *easy*," I groaned. "The hardest part is remaining still on my sofa. My hands want to wander all over the place right now."

"If that's what you feel like doing, don't let me stop you from enjoying the process. I encourage each of you to begin touching yourselves while you verbalize how you're feeling. Communication and openness are the first two essential ingredients in any healthy relationship."

As I watched Haley separate her legs further apart, I lifted my hand to my breast and squeezed it tightly while I lowered my other hand to my crotch and began to circle my button. Normally I'd take more time to tease myself, but at this point I was so horny I needed to get right down to business.

Watching me touch myself and begin to moan softly seemed to encourage Haley, as she moved her hand to the inside of her thighs and began to flutter her fingers over her button. While we both began to moan and roll our hips over our divans, Hannah began to bob her foot more forcefully over her knee and cleared her throat.

"Yes," she mewed. "It's a beautiful thing watching another woman pleasuring herself. Focus on one another as you listen to the reaction of your own body and that of your partner. The biggest turn-on is seeing your partner respond excitedly to your touch."

I wasn't sure if she was talking more about what *she* was feeling at this precise moment, or referring to what we were experiencing. It must have been even more exciting for her watching two sexy women touching their naked bodies only a few feet in front of her. With her special sex toy working its wonders underneath her business suit, I imagined she'd have experienced multiple climaxes facilitating these sessions.

"Don't forget to communicate how you feel," she said. "Tell your partner what she's doing to you right now."

"I'm so excited watching Jade touch herself," Haley said. "I never thought a woman could look this sexy and beautiful before. The feelings inside are even more intense than last time–"

"And *you*, Jade?" Hannah said. "How is your body responding seeing Haley get excited watching you?"

"Oh my God," I groaned. "I want her so bad. I want to touch her and taste her and feel her trembling in my arms."

"Soon enough," Hannah smiled. "For now, I just want you both to learn how to satisfy one another at a distance without the added pressure of direct engagement. Focus on what you're feeling, and surrender to the pleasure engulfing your bodies. As before, feel free to experiment with different forms of stimulation. You can begin learning from one another even before you come together."

I spread my legs further apart and inserted two fingers from my other hand into my hole as I began to rub my clit more quickly.

"Mmm, yes," I panted. "You're so beautiful, Haley. I'm imagining you touching me..."

"Yes, Jade," Haley said. "I want to touch you and feel your wetness. You're making me so hot right now."

Haley mimicked my technique, awkwardly inserting the middle finger of her left hand into her slit while she pumped it in and out as she began jilling herself more rapidly. Our hips began to slowly lift off our divans and our mouths opened in pleasure as we moved inexorably closer to orgasm.

"Yes, baby," I purred. "I want to watch you let it go. Imagine me sucking your jewel as you come in my mouth–"

"Oh God," Haley squealed as she arched her hips higher in the air. "It's *coming*! Suck my pussy, Jade!"

Suddenly, Haley fell back onto the surface of the divan and she hunched over, jerking her body back and forth while she pressed her fingers deeper inside her pussy. Seeing her come just inches away from me was more than I could take. I suddenly flipped over on all fours and pounded my cunt as my tits wobbled excitedly over my chest. Within seconds, my orgasm washed over me like a tidal wave as I began squirting long streams in Haley's direction. While I peered at her between my legs, I saw her mouth gape wider apart as she watched me writhing uncontrollably on the chair in front of her.

I glanced over at Hannah for a moment and saw her slumping rhythmically in her own chair as she watched the two of us cumming with our fingers deeply embedded in our pussies. I smiled, knowing she had her *own* special finger stimulating her G-spot as she surrendered to an entirely different kind of lover.

4

After we all came down from our highs at Hannah's therapy session, she asked Haley and me if we were ready to proceed to the next stage in our intimacy journey. Knowing this meant we'd be allowed to touch each other, we both quickly agreed, but since we'd used up all the allotted time in the day's session, Hannah scheduled our next meeting for the following week. When we parted, Haley and I kissed each other on the cheek, but that was enough to keep me going until we met next time.

In the intervening week, I ran through all kinds of scenarios imagining how I'd like to touch and caress her. It was kind of fun not using any toys for a change, since I knew those would be off base during our next encounter. Hannah didn't want any artificial stimulation getting in the way of Haley learning to enjoy sex in the natural manner. That was easy for *her* to say, I thought, remembering how she'd responded watching Haley and me writhing on our divans while she let her special sex toy do all the work for her. But I knew she was right, and as I lay on my sofa dreaming of all the ways I could stimulate Haley, I came many times remembering what she'd said to me when she experienced her first orgasm in the presence of another woman.

This time, I thought, *she won't need to pretend that I'm touching her when she comes next to me.*

On the day of our next scheduled session, we arrived at Hannah's office a few minutes early, which gave her a chance to prep us and set the ground rules. The most important thing, she said, was to go slow and make sure our partner felt comfortable before pushing any further.

I looked around her office and noticed that the two settees had been pushed to the side, and I looked at her inquisitively.

"Where did you want us to relax?" I asked.

Hannah smiled as she led us into another room with a four-poster bed. The drapes had been pulled and a series of candles were lit around the room to set the mood. I could smell a hint of lemongrass from some burning incense on the night table, and I nodded at Hannah's preparation.

"I thought you might like something a little more comfortable to relax on this time," she said. "Plus, I suspect you'll need a little more room to maneuver as you begin to explore each other's bodies. I wanted to make sure you felt as cozy as possible before proceeding to the next step. Why don't you give it a try and see what you think?"

I strolled up to the bed and ran my fingers over the linens. The high thread count made the bedding feel like silk, and I got goosebumps imagining what it would feel like to lie next to Haley on the sumptuous surface.

"What do you think, Haley?" I said. "Do you think this will be suitable for our purposes?"

Haley stepped forward and ran her hands over the sheets, then turned toward Hannah and smiled.

"It feels like I'm in a five-star hotel," she said. "I've never experienced anything so luxurious in my entire life."

"I wanted you to feel completely relaxed in preparation for the next step in your journey of sexual awakening."

"What about *you*?" Haley asked. "Where will you be while Jade and I are resting on the bed?"

Hannah turned to a reclining chair resting in the corner of the room.

"I'll be sitting in the shadows not too far away. I want there to be minimum distraction while you and Jade explore each other's bodies."

"So you'll be with us for the remainder of the session then?"

"If that's what you prefer."

"You were very helpful last time," Haley nodded. "Plus, it somehow seems more erotic knowing you'll be watching us."

Hannah paused as she peered at the two of us with a sly smile.

"I'll try to be less involved this time while I give each of you a chance to experiment with what turns you on. But I assure you that I'll be enjoying the process almost as much as you will."

She walked to the other side of the room and lay down in her chair, crossing her legs.

"To get you in the mood, sometimes it can be more exciting to let your partner take your clothes off before you lie down. Who'd like to begin?"

Haley and I peered at one another, and a blush fell over her cheeks. It was obvious that she wanted me to make the first move, which was fine with me since I'd been undressing her with my eyes from the moment we came in the door. She'd chosen to wear a more formal outfit today, with a collared blouse, wool pants, and suede loafers. Whether she was trying to mimic me or she was trying to project the image of more sophisticated woman, was unclear. Either way, I liked the look, and I felt my heart beating faster as I imagined unbuttoning her blouse.

I stepped forward and reached out my hand to her, and she met mine with her opposite hand, squeezing my fingers gently. I tilted my head down, and she closed her eyes, anticipating my kiss. Pausing an inch from her mouth, I felt her cool breath on my skin, and my pussy twitched when I realized I was about to touch her intimately for the first time.

When our lips touched, she puckered them like they used to in old-time movies. I smiled, realizing that this might have been the first romantic contact she'd ever experienced and that she still hadn't learned the art of erotic kissing. I lifted my hand and cupped her face as I moved closer, pressing my body against hers. She unconsciously tilted her pelvis, pressing her hips against mine. I parted my mouth and nibbled her flesh, feeling the fullness of her lips.

She sighed as we pressed our breasts together, and I circled my arm around her, caressing the indentation of her lower back. I was dying to plunge my tongue into her, but I remembered Hannah's admonition about going slowly, and instead I turned around and sat down on the bed with my knees straddling her hips. While Haley peered down at me, I began to loosen the buttons of her blouse from the top. As I began to spread the panels apart, I smiled when I noticed that she was wearing a lacy bra like the one I'd worn at our last session.

I leaned in and kissed her exposed belly with my moist lips, reaching up to cup her breasts as I squeezed them gently. She began to moan and reached behind my head to run her fingers through my hair. I'd almost forgotten how to properly make love a woman with all my recent escapades, and suddenly I was happy that I'd agree to participate in Hannah's guided session.

Maybe I'd needed this as much as Haley did.

As she pulled my head tighter against her belly, I reached behind her and unfastened the clasp at the back of her bra, pulling it gently over her shoulders. Her brassiere fell below her breasts, and I lifted myself up, licking her pointy tips. Her nipples were hard and warm, and as I sucked them into my mouth one at a time, she gasped, pulling my head harder against her body. As I began to roll my tongue over her tips, I moved my hands to the front of her chest and squeezed her breasts more tightly. They felt full and firm in my palms, and for the first time since I'd entered the office, I became conscious of the warm feeling in my pussy. My juices had been flowing for some time now, and the feeling of wetness between my legs made my nipples harden.

Haley was running her fingers through my hair more wildly now, and I took this to mean that she was ready for me to take it to the next step. I traced my hands down the front of her belly, unclasping the button at the top of her pants, then I slowly pulled the zipper down to reveal a pair of black lace panties. Seeing her wearing sexy lingerie got me even more turned on, and I slipped my fingers over the waist of her pants and began to pull them down over her hips.

My heart pounded as I felt them tighten up when they reached the widest part of her hips, realizing just how curvy and tight her ass must have been. As I pulled them further down her thighs, Haley lifted her feet and kicked off her loafers, stepping out of her jeans. I pulled her blouse off her back, and her brassiere fell softly onto the floor. Now she stood inches away from me, almost naked and quivering in excitement.

Hannah must have sensed Haley's trepidation, as I heard her shift in her chair for the first time and clear her throat.

"Sometimes it's even more erotic to have your partner remove her clothes while you *watch*," she said. "Would you like to undress Jade yourself Haley, or watch her do so herself?"

"I've been dreaming of seeing her naked again this whole week," Haley said. "But I'm not as experienced as Jade in the art of undressing another woman..."

Taking Haley's cue, I stood up off the bed and stepped back a few paces to give her a chance to take in my full figure. I smiled at her as I began to slowly unbutton my blouse. I'd decided to go braless for today's session, and as it became apparent to Haley that I was naked under my shirt, I saw her eyes widening in excitement. After I unclasped the fourth button, I let the silky fabric fall on top of my breasts while I breathed in and out deeply. As my nipples began to harden, pressing against the soft fabric, Haley's lips begin to separate.

I teased her for a moment longer, bringing my hands together and pushing my tits closer together. She panted looking at my cleavage, and I felt my pussy getting wetter seeing her rising excitement. When I undid the last button and threw my blouse on the bed beside me, I watched the flickering light casting sexy shadows over Haley's mounds. I wanted to step forward and trib her pointed nipples with my own, but I reminded myself that this session was all about her. The more slowly I could build her desire, the more I knew she'd enjoy the moment when we finally came together.

Damn, I thought. It had been a long time since I'd been this patient in seducing another woman. Apparently I needed Hannah's guided lessons just as much as Haley.

As we stood facing each other in the hypnotic shadows, Haley glanced down my midsection and a small curl formed on the side of her lips. For the same reason she'd chosen to dress more maturely, I'd chosen to wear jeans so she'd feel more comfortable seeing me as a peer. But the problem with the tight jeans was that they revealed the widening wet spot between my legs far more easily than when I wore my skirt.

"It looks like you're getting just as excited as me," Haley smiled, locking her eyes on my dark stain.

"Sorry," I shrugged. "I guess I lubricate a little more easily than most women."

"Mmm, I like that," Haley purred. "I can't wait to feel you. I'm beginning to get wet too."

I glanced down at Haley's legs and saw the shimmering slickness on the inside of her thighs.

"Perhaps it's time for the two of you to get more comfortable on the bed," Hannah interrupted from the darkness.

I'd almost forgotten she was there, but far from finding her intrusions irritating, I was glad she knew when we needed a little prompt. I slipped off my jeans, then lay down on the bed with my arm cocked sexily against the side of my head in a come-hither look to Haley. She didn't hesitate to join me on the other side of the bed, and we quickly melted into each other's arms. As I felt her press her body against mine, I kissed her with an open mouth, and this time she parted her lips and allowed my tongue to probe her cavity. Our breasts mashed together, and as we intertwined our legs, we both began to moan passionately. I pulled my leg up, pressing it against her pussy, and she responded by grinding her hips against my thigh.

By now, she'd joined me in thrusting her tongue into my mouth, and as we writhed together on the bed, I grabbed her ass and pulled her closer. The passion with which she was tongue-fucking me made me think she was ready for different kind of tongue lashing, and after a few minutes I disengaged and began nibbling my way down the front of her body. The only sound I could hear from the other sound of the room now was the soft rusting of Hannah shifting in her chair and the occasional soft sigh. I wondered if Haley sensed how much she was enjoying herself watching us, but at this point my only concern was satisfying the pretty girl lying beside me.

As I nibbled on Haley's teats and swirled my tongue over her areolas, she arched her back and pressed herself more firmly against me. It was apparent to me that she'd lost all of her inhibitions about being with another woman, and I hummed my approval as her body responded to my touch. I traced the little indentation running down the center of her tummy with my tongue, and her stomach quivered the closer I got to her private area as she began to roll her hips in anticipation of my touch.

When I reached her panties, I pulled them over her hips while she lifted her ass off the bed. Her bush felt as soft as fur and I rolled my cheeks over it, reveling in it's sexy scent and plush thickness. Beads of lubrication rested on her muff like morning dew on a spider web, and I paused to suck them into my mouth, tasting her sweet honey.

The further down I lowered myself, the further she spread her legs apart, until my shoulders were comfortably nestled between her legs. For a moment, I paused with my head cocked above her clit as I closed my eyes and inhaled her sweet, perfumy scent. After a few moments, she began to shimmy her hips impatiently, eager to feel my touch in her special place. Instead, I dribbled some saliva out of my mouth and let it fall on top of her inflamed jewel. When she felt the unexpected moisture on her button, she groaned and lifted her hips closer to my face.

"Oh God, Jade," she whined. "You're driving me crazy. I want to feel your touch so bad. Take me into your mouth like you said you would last time. Suck my pussy with your pretty mouth."

Her dirty talk just turned me on all the more, and I lowered my head to encircle her burning clit.

"Oh God–Oh God," Haley panted. "That feels so good. Lick my little man with your lips and make me feel like you did when I watched you last time."

Little man, I chuckled to myself. I hadn't heard that expression used by a woman before to describe her clit, and I wondered if this was a euphemism her parents had used when she was younger. But it didn't matter to me–I was just thrilled that she was expressing her desire for me and telling me how much I was turning her on.

As I hummed in delight, I began circling her button with the tip of my tongue, and she began groaning more loudly. While I mixed up my technique between sucking and licking her pearl, she placed her hands behind my head once again and pulled me harder into her crotch. As her breathing began to get more ragged and accelerated, I knew that she was getting close to the point of no return. I was tempted to pull back for a few seconds to prolong her torment, but then I realized there'd be plenty more time to tease and play with her after she released her pent-up sexual tension. She began to lift her hips off the bed as her body became rigid in a tight lock, and I slipped my fingers inside her and began to stroke her tenting G-spot.

"Oh God, Jade," she hissed. "Don't stop. I'm going to cum. *Yes!*" she grunted. "I'm cumming in your mouth!"

Suddenly, I felt the walls of her pussy clamping down on my fingers in rhythmic contractions as she humped her hips against my face while holding me tightly against her. I paused for a moment to feel her body spasming as I peered up and watched her pretty face contorting into paroxysms of pleasure. After what seemed like a full minute of tensing her body in a prolonged and powerful orgasm, she finally dropped her hips down onto the bed, panting loudly to catch her breath.

With the room suddenly quiet, I heard gentle squeaks coming

from the other side of the room as Hannah shifted rhythmically in her chair. It was obvious to both of us what was going on in the dark, and we smiled at one another as I pulled myself back up to look into Haley's steamy eyes.

"That was beautiful, Jade," she sighed. "Thank you for making me feel like a woman for the first time in my life. I can't believe how skilled a lover you are. I'm afraid that I'll never be able to meet your expectations–"

"Remember that there are no expectations or targets in this first direct encounter between the two of you," Hannah breathed deeply, collecting herself. "Jade–why don't you show Haley how she can satisfy you. Sometimes it's more fun for the *receiver* to take the lead."

I knew immediately what Hannah meant, and as I lifted myself up off the bed, I looked into Haley's eyes and nodded.

"Why don't you lie there for a little longer and let me do most of the work?" I said.

I raised myself up on all fours and straddled her face with my knees on either side of her head, and she looked up at me with wide eyes and smiled. As I ran my fingers gently through her silky hair, I began to lower myself until my dripping pussy hovered inches over her pouty lips. She flicked her tongue out awkwardly trying to bat my clit, and I cupped her cheeks, lowering myself a little further until my nub pressed against her lips.

"Just open your mouth a little bit and nibble on me for a moment," I said. "Sometimes when you're making love to a woman, less is more. Let me ease into it while I watch your pretty face."

Haley did as she was told, and as she sucked my hard nub into her mouth, I closed my eyes and groaned.

"Yes, baby," I purred. "Just like that. Suck my button and roll it around in your mouth. I like the feeling of your mouth on my body."

As Haley began to roll her tongue over my bulb in a similar manner to the way I'd kissed her earlier, I smiled. She was a quick study, and I felt myself growing closer to her with every passing moment.

"Yes, Haley," I encouraged her. "Just like that. Feel my hard clit in your mouth. I'm making love to your mouth while I watch you. I'm going to cum for you soon."

Haley's head nodded excitedly, and her eyes began to widen as I pressed my pussy harder down onto her face. I could feel the passion rising within me but I didn't want to drown her in another torrent if I came too hard, so as my orgasm began to take hold of me, I lifted my hips and pointed my pussy over her tits while I squirted my juices all over her heaving chest. As she peered down at me between my legs, I saw her face twist into another silent orgasm. Apparently, I'd excited her so much with my waterworks that she hadn't needed any direct stimulation to come once again.

As we both groaned and shook our bodies together on the bed, I heard the sound of gentle sloshing coming from the direction of Hannah's chair. I peered over at her and noticed that her pants were unbuttoned while she rubbed her hands sensuously over her naked mound.

"That was very good, ladies," she sighed. "You're making excellent progress. It's time for the last step in your pair bonding. Now I want you to touch each other at the same time and experience the joy of coming together. Jade, I'm guessing you have a bit more experience in this area."

"Perhaps just a little," I smiled, as I shimmied my hips over Haley's slippery torso toward her quivering pussy. I paused for a moment when I reached her bush once again and tilted my pelvis back and forth over top of her bush, feeling the soft hairs tickling my clit and wet opening.

"Would you like me to make love to you now, Haley?" I purred.

"Isn't that what we've been doing all this time?" she said.

"Not quite *this* way," I smiled. "I think you might find this brings us even closer together and feels even more amazing. Lift your knees up higher and spread your legs for me."

Haley looked at me confused for a moment, and I nodded reassuringly. When she pulled her knees almost up to her chest, I pushed her thighs apart and peered at her inflamed gland, poking its head out of its hood. I kneeled over top of her and slowly lowered my body until the bottom of our thighs rested on one another. Her eyes widened when she realized what I intended to do, and a sly smile formed on my mouth as our clits touched for the first time. As I began to grind our hips together providing direct stimulation to our most sensitive areas, she threw her head back and groaned . I didn't know if she'd even conceived of two women touching themselves this way, but the look of pleasure on her face indicated that she was quickly losing herself in the process.

As I shifted my weight forward and back, stroking her hard clit and rubbing our sopping pussies together, she began to whimper and toss her head from side to side. Seeing her enjoying the tribbing action so much just made me want to fuck her harder. I transferred more of my weight onto her thighs, and she began to rock her hips in concert with mine. The feeling of our nubs rolling over one another as our slits smacked against one another was the most exciting feeling either one of us had experienced. Before long, she began moaning more urgently, and I saw a flush begin to spread over her chest as her nipples contracted even more firmly.

"Yes, Haley," I groaned, seeing the look of ecstasy roll over her face. "Let it go baby. Let me feel you cum with me while I make love to you."

"Yes, Jade," Haley grunted. "I feel it coming. I'm going to cum so hard against your pussy. Fuck me harder."

That was all I needed to hear as I pressed my hips harder down onto her vulva and began humping her more forcefully. When I heard her pussy begin to make sexy gassy sounds, I knew she was cumming again, but this time I stayed connected to her while my own orgasm took hold of me. The sound of my juices spraying onto her gaping hole as she moaned in euphoria was the sexiest thing I'd ever heard. As we came together listening to the sound of our pussies spasming in the height of ecstasy, I leaned forward and kissed her passionately. Haley had come a long way since her first awkward guided session with Hannah, and as our pussies continued twitching against one another, we both sighed in contentment.

Soon after, we heard Hannah moaning softly in her chair, and we turned our heads to see that she'd pulled her pants down all the way and was ramming her long dildo in and out of her pussy.

"I'd have to say you've both graduated with flying colors," she panted as her body jerked softly in her chair.

Haley and I looked at each for a moment with the same thought, nodding our heads in Hannah's direction.

"I think maybe Hannah needs a little therapy session of her *own* now," I smiled.

Want more all-girl erotic chills and thrills? Download the next volume in the discounted collection:

No boys allowed...

Sneak peek:

As I began to feel the sweat dripping over my forehead and the pleasure spreading throughout my body, I slowly lowered my raised leg and spread my thighs apart, showing the girl my dripping pussy. She grabbed one of her tits with her free hand and pinched her long nipple while she stared at my glistening snatch. Before long, both of us were moaning softly, jilling ourselves with increasing fervor...

READ MORE

MORE FROM VICTORIA RUSH:

Choose your next toe-curling fantasy from over thirty-five spicy stories in Jade's Erotic Adventures. Browse the full collection here:

Click to scan your favorites...

FOLLOW VICTORIA RUSH:

Want to keep informed of my latest erotic book releases? Sign up for my newsletter and receive a FREE bonus book:

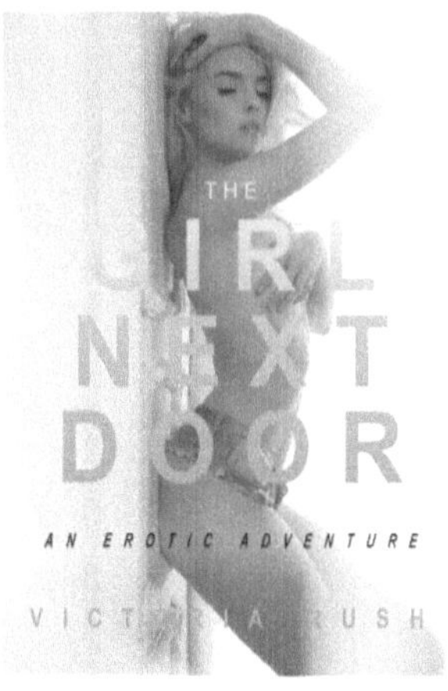

Spying on the neighbors just got a lot more interesting...